To JANO,

Devoted

Hope to know you
for many more
years to come!

Alise R Solomon

by

Alison R. Solomon

Wild Girl Press

Copyeditor: Nann Dunne
Interior Design: Patty Schramm
Cover Design: Tree House Studio

Published in the United States by Wild Girl Press

ISBN: 978-0-9984400-0-2
eISBN: 978-0-9984400-1-9

Dedication

To my mother, Irene Rivka Trenner

I always knew how lucky I was to have a mother with such a gentle soul and adventurous spirit

Acknowledgements

I am filled with gratitude to the following people who helped me bring this novel to fruition:

Darla Baker, Chris Paynter and Suzie Carr for your unstinting advice and support.

Erin Saluta and Franci McMahon for slogging through early versions of this novel and Barbara Clanton, for taking on the later version. Special thanks to Jenny Harmon who read both the earlier and later versions of Devoted.

My sister, Vivienne, for your very thorough proofreading.

Nann Dunne for your excellent editing.

Ann McMan for your flawless cover.

Patty Schramm for your formatting expertise.

My amazing wife, Carol Farrell, for your constant support and guidance.

I am so lucky to live in Gulfport, which shows its support to the LGBTQ community in so many ways. If any of you are looking for a safe, inclusive and warm place to live, check out our community.

PART ONE

ASHLEY

Chapter One

The call comes in the early morning. I jump, and the tea I'm drinking spills into the saucer. It's my sister's wife, JP.

"Lizzie's in the E.R."

My heart plummets. "Again? I can get on a plane this morning. Should I come?"

"No. It'll probably be like last time. I'll call you as soon as I have any news. I have to get off the phone. They're not allowed in here."

"JP, I—" But the line's dead. When I pick up my tea, my hand is trembling.

§♦

Twelve months ago, I received a different phone call that set me shaking. Lizzie told me she'd been diagnosed with FSGS: Focal Segmental Glomerulosclerosis.

"What the heck is that?"

"It's a form of kidney disease."

I was stupefied. Lizzie was the picture of health, constantly eating the healthiest foods and working out regularly. But she hadn't always been. Before she left California, she was a drunk: plowing her car into the neighbor's front yard, getting fired for constant tardiness, slurring on the phone. She sobered up when she moved to Philadelphia, but was it too late?

"I thought alcohol affected the liver, not the kidneys."

"It's not connected to the drinking. They don't know why I have it."

"How serious is it?" I asked.

"It's a chronic disease. It could ultimately lead to kidney failure, but—"

"Oh my God! What can I do?" I was ready to jump on

the next plane and donate an organ, if that was what she needed.

"Calm down, Ash." Lizzie's voice was soft and reassuring. "It *could* lead to kidney failure way into the future, but Doctor Marshall thinks he caught it early enough. With treatment I should be asymptomatic for years."

"If you don't have any symptoms, why were you even seeing the doctor?"

"Routine blood tests. They spotted a pattern they'd never noticed before."

"You mean you've had it for years?" I had so many questions, I didn't even know where to start. "Should I come visit? I could get off work..."

"No. I have JP. She's going to take very good care of me. Not that there's anything to do now, anyway."

I sighed. I sometimes felt as if JP and I were in competition when it came to Lizzie. I could picture JP standing in the background shaking her head at my offer to visit.

"I'll be praying for you, sis. I'm going to put you on the prayer list at church too, so everyone can pray for you."

"That's sweet, Ash, but don't get overdramatic. It's not cancer or anything."

"I can't help it. You're my baby sister. I don't want anything to happen to you, ever."

She laughed. "I know. You're the best big sister anyone could have. But don't worry. I lead a great life and have a wonderful partner. Nothing's going to happen to me."

ॐ

But something *has* happened, and it's not the first time. Last month Lizzie was hospitalized overnight because of dizziness and nausea. They discharged her the next day with a clean bill of health, and we all breathed a sigh of relief.

Now she's back in the E.R. again.

Should I ignore JP's advice and head out to Philly? I'm her big sister. I should be there to protect her. But JP's her wife, and I know she'll move heaven and earth to make sure Lizzie's well taken care of.

I have to get ready for work, but figuring out what to wear is the last thing on my mind. I pull a grey, wool dress off the hanger and slip into black pumps. When I check my hair in the mirror, the figure staring back at me looks like she's dressed for a funeral. I tear the dress off and shrug on a bright red one instead. *She'll be fine. Just like last time.*

The drive to my job at Grace Covenant School is a short one. This time of year I usually keep an eye out for late-lying snow or early almond blossoms, but today I see nothing. Once at work, I stay in my office as much as possible and try to catch up on emails, avoiding kids who might want to   interact with me. But I can't concentrate. I feel so powerless. By lunchtime, I make an excuse and skip out early.

At home, I sit on the sofa, clasp my hands together, and offer up silent prayers.

"Superstitious hogwash, Ash." I can hear Lizzie's voice as clearly as if she were sitting by my side. "Religious mumbo-jumbo."

It's amazing how she went from one extreme to the other with her faith. She was the one who recruited high school students to take a virginity pledge. The one who said her goal in life was to marry a good man and have lots of kids. Once she met JP, all that went out the window. She didn't just abandon her church, she actively despised it.

For me, it's more complicated. Sometimes I do feel confined by my religion, but I worry that without it, I'd have nothing. After our parents died, I felt so alone. Activities like singing in the church choir and serving meals at the shelter keep me grounded and give me a sense of family, especially now that   Lizzie lives so far away.

The phone rings and I almost drop it in my anxiety to grab onto it.

"JP?" I ask, even though I can see the caller ID. "Is Lizzie doing better?"

"No." I wait for more information, but none is forthcoming.

"How bad is it?"

"She's going downhill fast."

"Downhill? Dear God, what's going on?" I push the words out with all the force I can muster, thinking they will come out as an almighty roar, but all that comes out is a high-pitched squeak. "Her kidneys have shut down." Her voice sounds muffled as if she may be trying not to cry. "If you want to see her, you better get on a plane tonight." I feel as if I've been punched in the gut. "Tonight? But surely..." I trail off, waiting for JP to soften the blow. She says nothing.

That's when I know for sure what she's telling me: my beloved baby sister Lizzie, who celebrated her thirty-third birthday barely six months ago, is dying.

ᔥ

The red-eye flight is grueling, especially since it involves a layover. I try to read *The Shack,* which I grabbed from the shelf on my way out the door, but I can't concentrate. Older sisters are meant to protect their siblings, and I'd do anything to save Lizzie. I don't understand how the doctors could have said she was fine, and a month later, her kidneys have shut down.

I should have jumped on a plane this morning. Why did I   listen to JP? Ever since our parents died, I've been second-guessing myself: What's best for Lizzie? How can I keep her safe? The guilt that's never far away, settles on my shoulders like a hundred pound barbell.

I need to sleep, but when I close my eyes, my mind conjures up endless images of Lizzie and me together: playing hopscotch in front of Gran's house, driving her to the prom when she wore that ridiculous lime taffeta, shoving piles of her clothes into the trunk of my car when she finally left Kurt.

Those pictures get superimposed on that dreadful day we lost our parents, and I have to pull my thoughts away because I can't bear to remember the funeral and the aftermath. When I steer my memory in a different direction, it takes me to that first meeting with JP, the mistake I made, and how I feel as if I've been apologizing ever since.

I still can't believe Lizzie could be dying. Maybe I'll arrive and learn that it was all a mistake, her kidneys have recovered, or she's received a transplant. Surely they'll tell

she's on the mend and will be out of the hospital in
r so.

he Philadelphia airport I text JP and hurry to the
bathroom to brush my teeth and apply some makeup.
There are dark shadows under my eyes, and my skin is
even whiter than usual. My mousy hair looks dank, as if it
hasn't been washed in a week. I pull back stray strands of
hair that have come loose and shove them into my
ponytail.

"You have such lovely hair, why do you restrain it?"
Lizzie used to ask, until she gave up trying to get me to
change.

"I have to keep it under control." I believe my hair
mirrors my state of being. Sometimes I wish I could let go
of things more—my hair, my eating habits, the religious
strictures I impose on myself—but I'm scared that if I do,
everything will fall apart. So I keep my hair tightly pulled
back, and I wear clothes that fit my angular body without
emphasizing any part of it. Nothing too tight and nothing
loose or free flowing. I've never cared about fashion
trends, as long as I look neat and tidy. I was one of those
kids who was sorry to stop wearing a uniform when I got to
high school, and if I could still wear a white short-sleeved
blouse with blue shorts every day, I'd be happy.

People say Lizzie and I look alike. We're both average
height, long-waisted, and our legs are muscled from
running. We have Mom's blue eyes and a cleft in our chin
from Dad. The similarities end there though. Lizzie's silky,
chestnut hair falls in waves around her face, her
cheekbones are soft, and she has a little snub nose. My
cheekbones are high, my noise too pointy, and my thin lips
make me look severe, even when I smile. Does my
appearance reflect my personality or is it vice versa? If I
looked more like Lizzie, would I have softened up like her?
If only I could find a way to loosen up, but still hold
everything together.

This morning my gaunt face appears more austere than
ever. I methodically apply eye shadow to my eyelids. I know
it's crazy, but it's a habit. I've always presented myself to
Lizzie and the world as well put together, and I'm not going
to change now. What if she doesn't know how dire her
situation is? My not wearing makeup would say it all.

JP is leaning against her pickup truck in the arrivals zone, looking impatient. Her hair is so short she seems almost bald. A shapeless plaid shirt hangs from her shoulders, and her baggy cargo shorts have settled loosely below her hips. She's lost weight since I saw her a couple of years ago. If I didn't know   better, I'd think she was the one with the medical disorder.

"You texted five minutes ago. The security guys were trying to move me on."

"I'm sorry." I throw my overnight bag onto the jump seat of the pickup. As usual, I'm starting out by apologizing to JP. I settle into the passenger seat, and she pulls away from the curb.

She doesn't ask how the flight was, so I break the silence. "Tell me again what the doctors are saying."

"There's not much to tell. They don't know why she deteriorated so suddenly." She stares directly ahead of her and steers the pickup onto the freeway. JP has never been chatty, but her silence is frustrating. I try again. "Last year she told me this form of kidney disease would be totally manageable. So what happened?" I swivel in my seat and pull my safety belt to the side so I can look right at her.

"Your guess is as good as mine. Did the doctors mess up? After all, they missed her condition for years. All those times she went to the doctor because of blood in her urine, they insisted it coincided with her period. The fact that her protein levels were high? They brushed it off."

"Maybe we shouldn't have put such faith in their optimism and researched it ourselves."

JP keeps her gaze on the road. "We could've gone crazy researching on the Internet, but when all the doctors tell you not to worry, you don't. Especially if you're Lizzie."

I nod. Lizzie was never one to make a fuss. Over the past year I've tried to ask her whether she thought her doctor was negligent in not picking up on the FSGS sooner, but she wouldn't go there with me.

"Okay, I'll level with you. She brought it on herself," JP says.

"*What?*" I swivel back around to face JP. Her gaze doesn't stray from the road.

"The docs think it was the alcohol that caused the kidney failure."

7

"But why now? Lizzie is ten years sober."

"I'm sorry to break this to you, Ash, but she wasn't. In the last year, she kept having slips, some worse than others."

"Slips?" Surely Lizzie would have told me if she'd fallen off the wagon. She'd been so upfront with me, once she recognized her addiction. "She never said anything."

JP shrugs. "She looked up to you. She didn't want to disappoint you. There were all kinds of things she didn't share with you."

"What things?"

JP doesn't answer. She maneuvers the pickup off the freeway.

We're in an area I'm not familiar with, nowhere near center city. Somehow I'd assumed she'd be at one of the prestigious city hospitals.

I'm still struggling with the idea that my sister had slips. "I don't believe Lizzie would have compromised her sobriety."

"It wasn't the first time. She had a slip a year ago, when she was first diagnosed. The other night when I brought her into the E.R., she had come home completely smashed."

"A year ago? Two nights ago...are you sure?"

"Jesus, Ashley, ask Paula about last year if you don't believe me." Paula is Lizzie's best friend. "As for this time around, ask the doctors or nurses. They'll confirm what I said."

I sit back in silence, gazing out the window, seeing nothing.

It's hard to imagine Lizzie not telling me that she had a slip, even harder to believe she was drunk when she was admitted to the hospital. But JP has no reason to lie. Maybe Lizzie didn't confide in me; maybe she thought I'd find fault. After she gave up her faith, she kept trying to show me how my beliefs made me judge others. She said I was a good person, but that I had to start thinking for myself.

JP pulls into the driveway of a large, old-fashioned, brick building, nothing like the modern glass-and-steel structures hospitals tend to be nowadays.

"Why don't I drop you here and go park? She's on the

second floor. I told them you'd be coming."
I run through the double doors and follow the signs to the elevators. A desultory group of people is waiting, and now that I'm so close, I'm too desperate to see Lizzie to wait. I push open the small door next to the elevators and take the stairs two at a time, vaguely registering the plain white concrete steps, the paint peeling off the walls. I pull open the heavy door onto the second floor and head toward the nurses' station.

A plump, middle-aged woman, whose Afro frames her face like a halo, asks how she can help me. When I tell her who I am, she looks relieved and hurries me down the hall.

Inside Lizzie's room, it's hard to believe the woman propped up in the hospital bed is my sister. Her skin is yellow and she's so bloated she reminds me of one of those blimps that hover in the sky, encouraging me to buy their brand of beer or insurance. An oxygen mask covers her nose and mouth and an IV snakes itself around her arm. Her eyes are closed.

I tiptoe over and stand at the bedside.

"Lizzie?" I whisper and stroke her swollen fingers. "Lizzie?"

I don't know if she can hear me, so I take a chance and say loudly, "It's me, Ash, your sister."

Her lids flutter and for a moment she opens her eyes. Her gaze is blank, and she closes her eyes again. Through the plastic of the oxygen mask, the corner of her mouth turns upward as if she's trying to smile. I squeeze her hand and she grimaces.

"I love you," I say, "darling, darling sister. I love you so much." I clench my throat tight to hold back a sob trying to make its way out.

My hand is in hers and she tries to lift it. I'm not sure if she wants to kiss my fingers. The effort is too much and her hand falls back. I lean forward and kiss her forehead. Maybe she wants to say something. I move the oxygen mask away from her face. She opens her mouth, but no sound comes out. She swallows and tries again, gasping for air. I lean forward to replace the oxygen mask, but she shakes her head.

"JP," she whispers, and I feel my heart constrict. I thought she'd be happy to see me. Apparently, the only person she wants next to her is her wife.

"She's coming. She's parking the truck."

She shakes her head with surprising vehemence and opens her eyes. They're no longer glazed or blank, only full of agitation. She's trying to get a sentence out, but it's barely a mumble and there are only a couple of words I can catch. "JP...affair...Jim..."

"JP had an affair with a guy called Jim?" It's about the most unlikely thing she could tell me, and I wonder what drugs they have her on. I stroke her hand, her forehead, any part of her I can touch. "Whatever happened, we don't need to talk about that now, honey, it doesn't matter."

"No...me." She gasps, then continues. "JP...mad."

Is this a deathbed confession? While I can't believe JP would have an affair with a guy, it's hard to imagine loyal, dependable Lizzie having an affair with anyone, female or male.

"Sweetheart, none of it matters. We're both here for you. We love you. She's parking the truck, she's not mad at you."

"Not now, then...she..." She sucks in all the air she can then forces out a string of words, mumbling and incoherent. "I told her...Hell and...in the water...no energy...drink...Jim...but I wasn't..."

"Lizzie, honey, I don't understand what you're trying to tell me. I'm sure it doesn't matter now." She's clearly exhausted, fighting for breath. I put the oxygen mask back over her nose and mouth.

Did I hear her say the word Hell? Is she saying she's going to Hell? I know she gave up her faith, but now that she's dying, is she clinging to it?

I wonder if there's a chaplain or pastor here. Even though Lizzie says she's no longer a Christian, she might want someone to pray with her and help her go home to God. I want to ask her, and yet she's already so upset and agitated, I don't want to make things worse. Does she understand how serious her condition is?

"Shall we pray together?" I stroke her hand. With a strength I would never have expected, she rips the mask off her face.

"Ash!" Her eyes, so empty a few moments ago, are burning fiercely.

"Yes, my sweet sister, I'm—" She cuts me off.

"JP!"

I turn, thinking JP is by the door or has come in. She hasn't. Lizzie's eyes grow wide and frantic. "Jim..." Again, something I can't make out, and then a word that sounds like prison.

"Jim is in prison?"

She shakes her head and pushes out the word one more time. It still sounds like she's saying prison, yet I know it's not quite that. Her mouth moves but nothing happens. All of a sudden she slumps. Her eyes roll backwards, and all the machines she's attached to start beeping frantically.

A nurse yells, "Code blue!" and there's a flurry of activity. I know it's too late. I've watched enough TV to know what it means when the machines show flat lines. Lizzie's chest is no longer rising and falling, and I can feel death in the air.

"*Lizzie!*" I spin around. JP stands in the doorway, stunned. She rushes into the room but Lizzie is now surrounded by medical professionals pumping on her chest, blowing some sort of balloon into her mouth, and JP can't get near her.

There is silence while the medical team works on Lizzie, and I hear the words, "Time of death..."

JP looks around in bewilderment, chokes up, and bursts into tears. She slides down onto the floor and I slide next to her. All I can think is that my sister is gone forever. I'm completely alone in the world. How can this have happened? How can my beloved sister, so healthy until last month, be dead?

Lizzie's last words echo over and over in my brain: Jim. Prison. All of a sudden, in the midst of my grief, the word comes unbidden into the forefront of my brain.

Poison.

She wasn't saying that Jim was in prison. With her dying breath, my sister was trying to tell me that someone named Jim had poisoned her.

Chapter Two

We remain slumped on the floor, JP and I, while the nurses fuss around Lizzie's body.

"Did she say anything before she...?" JP whispers.

What should I say? Should I tell her Lizzie admitted having an affair and that she was worried JP was mad at her? What about her final words? If Jim is the guy she had the affair with, how can I mention that Lizzie thinks he poisoned her?

JP has an expression of hope in her eyes. She wants to hear that Lizzie's last words were ones of love. I don't want to lie, but I can't bear to let JP down either.

"She repeated your name several times." I put my hand over hers.

"Did she say anything else?"

"She was struggling to talk."

JP nods. "She hadn't been able to say anything when I last saw her. Could you tell if she was happy to see you?" JP looks into my eyes, her expression a mix of anxiety and defeat.

"I think so, but honestly I don't know. She was a little agitated."

"Agitated? How?"

"I thought—I thought she might be trying to tell me something." JP's eyes grow so big that I can't help but reassure her. "She wanted to say how much she loved you. Perhaps she wanted to tell me that too, only she couldn't get the words out. Mostly I just held her hand."

JP nods. She looks so mournful that my heart goes out to her.

The nurse who guided me to Lizzie when I arrived comes over to us.

"Let me help you up," she says holding her hands out, one to each of us. "You can say your farewells."

Her lilting accent, which for a moment takes me far away to Kenya or Nigeria, is both strong and soothing. She indicates that I should go first and helps JP to a tired-looking plastic chair in the far corner of the room while I approach Lizzie. They've removed all the tubes and machines, so she's unencumbered in the bed. I stand over her, unable to believe that this has really happened. Who will I be in this world with no parents and no   sister? I wish I could believe that she's at peace, but I remember how agitated she looked in her dying moments. I sit on the side of the bed and pull her into my chest, hugging her fiercely. How is it possible that she will never hug me back?

"You were such a good person, darling sis. I'm sure you're safe in Jesus' loving arms," I tell her. Behind me I sense JP stiffen. She hates any mention of our faith. I move closer to Lizzie and put my lips toward her ear so no one else can hear. "I don't know what you were trying to tell me, darling sister, but I'll do whatever it takes to figure it out. Whoever Jim is, I'll bring him to justice."

I move away from the bed so JP can say her goodbyes. I leave the room and wander aimlessly down the corridor.

My mind is all over the place. I'm still reeling from the idea that Lizzie is no longer on this earth. I keep reliving that conversation when she told me that even with FSGS she would be healthy for years. How can a healthy thirty-three-year-old get this sick so quickly? JP says it was the alcohol. But did Lizzie really relapse?

"Can I help you?" I've stopped at the nurses' station and I'm leaning on the counter opposite a slim young nurse with skin the color of rich coffee.

"I'm Lizzie Glynn's sister."

She doesn't offer her condolences, so obviously her screen hasn't updated yet.

I try to think quickly through the thick fog that's pervaded my brain. "Did they do lab tests on my sister when she was first brought into the E.R.?"

The girl clicks and scrolls, moving the screen with her finger until she finds what she wants.

"Yes. They ordered tests to confirm acute renal

failure." She continues scrolling. "I see she was here a month ago. Everything was way worse this time."

"What about a tox screen? Did they do that too?"

"They didn't need to. She was admitted in a state of intoxication, clutching a bottle of vodka."

So it's true. She really had been drinking.

"I guess we'll have to wait for an autopsy to find out if there was any other substance inside her," I say. The young nurse looks shocked; it sounds as if I'm wishing death on my sister. "Lizzie died a few minutes ago." I choke up as I walk away.

JP and the nurse come out of Lizzie's room.

"I'll bag up Lizzie's belongings." The nurse motions for JP to follow her to a cubicle by the nurses' station. "There are various forms for you to sign."

I tag along behind. "Is there anything I can do to help?"

JP looks at me through eyes that are red and watery. "There's nothing anyone can do to help," she says. She turns away and I hear her mutter under her breath, "Though you could stop bringing up your damn religion."

I wait while she signs various forms.

"Do we know how quickly they'll get the autopsy done?" I ask. "I'd like to stay in town for the funeral."

"I already asked," JP says. "There won't be an autopsy. There's no need."

I'm surprised and I can't help wondering if this tired, old hospital really knows what it's doing. "I know this is hard for you—for both of us—but we have to be logical. We should push for an autopsy." Although JP is her wife, doesn't a sister have any say?

"Why do we need one? What good would it do?"

"It would give us some peace of mind as to why she died so suddenly."

JP sighs. "I already told you. When someone has a kidney disease and they go out and get drunk, that's all it takes sometimes."

"But..." I want to say, *but what if someone forced her to drink?* Except even if they did, an autopsy wouldn't show that. All it would show was whether she had alcohol in her system. I can't prove anything. Should I mention Jim, and what Lizzie said? JP's face is haggard. She looks so fragile, I can't bring it up.

"Would you like me to organize the church service?" I ask as JP picks up a form to sign. She stops and whirls around to face me. "Stop it, Ash! There won't be a church service. Lizzie wasn't a Christian."

"I know she wasn't religious anymore. I think maybe...right at the end...I feel so guilty that she didn't have a chaplain pray with her." JP slams her hand down on the form she's signing. "Lizzie would *not* have wanted the chaplain. And since she hadn't set foot inside a church in a decade, a service would be inappropriate."

JP turns the form over, but I can see she's not really reading it.

"If you don't have a service, what kind of funeral will it be?"

JP hands the form over to the clerk, and the clerk hands her a large plastic bag.

"Lizzie wanted to be cremated. It'll be private, though you can be there if you want."

I feel let down. I wish I'd had a chance to find out what Lizzie might have wanted. She used to be such a spiritual person. "A funeral is for everyone, not only for the person who's passed. You and Lizzie had lots of friends and it might help them. I know it would help me. I know you're hurting, so let me organize it."

All of a sudden JP looks so mad, she may be ready to take a swing at me. The nurse grabs her around the shoulder, as if she's trying to hug her, though she may be trying to stop my sister-in-law from lunging at me. JP points her finger at my face, so close to my eyes that I have to stand back so she doesn't poke them.

"Churches like yours wouldn't even recognize our relationship. Ten years ago you probably *would* have been able to take charge. Times have changed and the State recognizes that I'm Lizzie's wife, and if I say there'll be no funeral, then..." She stops to emphasize each word in turn, pointing her finger for emphasis. "There. Will. Be. No. Funeral." She picks up the plastic bag with Lizzie's effects in it and storms off down the hall.

I look at the nurse and raise my eyebrows, shocked by JP's behavior.

"She's upset, dear. It's not uncommon."

I'm upset too. I wish I could fall on the nurse's ample bosom and cry my eyes out. Instead, I turn around and walk outside.

There's no sign of JP so I figure perhaps she's meandering around the hospital grounds to give herself time to calm down. It's a cool, crisp day, and I pull my jacket tight around me. When I left California, it was hard to imagine it could be this cold this late in spring. The sky is bright, and that makes me feel a little better, knowing Lizzie left this world on such a glorious day. I couldn't have borne if it had been cloudy and raining.

I walk over to the parking lot, but I have no idea where JP parked, so I go back indoors. My head is throbbing. I haven't had anything to eat or drink since I arrived. I can't bear the thought of food so I buy a cup of black coffee. I wait for JP to call or text. I can't stop thinking about Lizzie's last words, the sentences she was trying to say. While I'm waiting, I write them all down. Maybe later, I'll be able to make sense of it. After two cups of coffee JP still hasn't texted, so I dial her cell phone. She doesn't answer so I text her. She doesn't reply to that either.

I pull out a book of meditations, but my heart's not in it. I keep picturing Lizzie as she was when we were children—laughing, playful, so full of life—and Lizzie as I saw her this morning, barely recognizable as my sister.

Just when I'm wondering what I should do next, my cell phone rings.

"I'm sorry I lost it with you," JP says.

"Where are you?" I ask.

"I drove home. I shouldn't have. I was shaking all the way. I was wrong to leave you there, but I don't think I should come back out. Take a cab here and I'll pay the fare."

"Don't worry about it. I'll see you shortly."

JP's always been a tough cookie: quick to anger and quick to forgive. Prickly on the outside but soft in the middle. She makes all her decisions with her heart, whereas I'm someone who takes pride in using my head and staying calm. *Lizzie has a little of both of us in her. Had.* I feel the tears well up, and this time I allow them to flow freely. I'll have to give my emotions a little space if I'm to return to my usual rational self. Because that's what

I have to do if I'm going to help give Lizzie the homecoming she deserves. And then find out what really caused her death.

Chapter Three

Before I get in the cab, I buy a large bouquet of flowers, white roses with a spray of tiny purple stars that the hospital volunteer tells me are called Trachelium. I give the cab driver the address and hope he's taking me the most direct route. I've never been able to get my bearings in this large city. JP and Lizzie bought the house a couple of years ago as a renovation project so I've only seen pictures of it online. When the trees are in bloom the street must be green and leafy, but they're still bare and the area looks forlorn and stark. Finally we stop outside a large, rambling house framed by enormous oak trees. The dark-blue pickup is parked out front.

I make my way up the path, and when I ring the front door bell, I'm assailed by a long-forgotten melody: Westminster Chimes. Tears spring to my eyes. It's an old English melody that my grandmother and Mom loved so much, and it's the same door chime we had growing up. I picture me and Lizzie racing to the front door from the school bus, vying to be the first to reach the bell. Mom always came to the door singing her accompaniment to the chime, and we would barrel into her to receive our hugs.

No one answers so I ring again. This time I picture us both racing to the front door to open it for Daddy after he came home from work.

I'm startled from my reverie when the door opens and a very large, pleasant-faced woman with wide-set green eyes and tumbling red curls that frame her face appears.

"This is Lizzie's house, isn't it?" I stumble, "I mean, JP's?"

"Yes." She nods. "You must be Ash. Come in, dear." She pulls me inside.

"I can't believe how much you and Lizzie look alike."
Her voice catches. "Looked... I'm so very sorry for your
loss. I'm Paula, Lizzie's best friend."

She plants her arms around me, hampered by the
flowers, and I have an immediate sense of wanting to put
the bouquet down so I can let this woman envelop me in
her warmth. Instead I stand with one foot twisted behind
my leg, and say, "I'm sorry for your loss too. I know you
loved Lizzie."

She ushers me down a hallway and into the kitchen.
Before we enter she whispers, "JP's a mess. I'm glad I
came when I did, but I won't stay long, now that you're
here."

JP is sitting at the table, her hands cupped around a
steaming mug. Her face is splotchy and her eyes, red. My
heart goes out to her and I thrust the flowers toward her.

She looks up at me, and the expression in her eyes is
one of defeat. "I'm sorry, Ash," she says. "I apologize for
how I acted. I know you loved Lizzie, and I know how
important your faith is to you. Maybe we can figure
something out."

Paula takes the flowers. "I'll just put these in a vase,
and then I'll leave you two alone." She busies herself with
cutting the cellophane and shaking the food powder into a
jug of water.

After Paula lets herself out, JP continues to sit at the
table, while I stand awkwardly to her side.

"I brought your suitcase in from the truck," she says at
last.

"Thanks."

I stir the cup of chai tea Paula made me before she left.
"I'm going to need to call work and tell them how long I'll
be off."

JP stares at me, uncomprehending, then realizes what
I'm asking.

"I'm not willing to do a funeral. We can have some of
our closest friends come over tomorrow and hold a
memorial."

"Here?" It's not what I pictured. "So soon?"

"Yeah. No need to wait. I already asked Paula if she'll
organize it. She's Jewish. They do their memorials pretty
swiftly, so she's done it before."

I feel my stomach tighten. Perhaps my face does too, because JP adds quickly, "I'm sure you can talk to Paula and add in a prayer or a reading."

I wish we didn't have to make these decisions in such a hurry. I know enough to realize that JP's in complete shock and not thinking straight. If only she'd agree to do something in a few weeks' time, I could work on a proper service.

"How about we have a small memorial tomorrow, and then something in a month or so. I could fly back..."

JP shakes her head. "Don't push your luck, sis-in-law. I'm giving you more than I would have wanted. If it were up to me, there'd be nothing. I'd sit in a room and bang my head against a wall for a week."

I can't bear that she's so distraught. I wish she understood how the rituals for grief are there to help us through times like this.

"Feel free to look around and see if there's anything of Lizzie's you want." JP gets up from the kitchen table. "I'm going into the garden."

Lizzie loved her garden. We both love being outdoors and in nature. Ugh, there I go again, thinking about her in the present. But how do you shift someone so quickly into the past tense? I can't stop thinking about Lizzie's last words and what she was trying to tell me. She definitely said she was having, or had, an affair. And right there I'm stumped, because Lizzie was the most loyal person I know. When she was married to Kurt, she wouldn't hear a word against him.

"He has a difficult job. It keeps him awake," she'd say when he came into the room sniffing, his eyes dilated after he'd clearly taken a hit of cocaine.

"He didn't mean it. He doesn't know better," was her excuse when he belittled her.

When she finally left, she told me it was because she was becoming her worst self. "A partner should help you be your best self. Kurt couldn't do that. I had to leave, not before *he* got worse. Before *I* did."

I remember that so distinctly. She knew what she wanted and needed in a partner, and even though I found it hard to accept at first, I always thought she'd found what she needed in JP.

JP said Lizzie had started drinking again. But why? Lizzie only drank when she was with Kurt. In the hospital, Lizzie said something about having no energy. Was she using alcohol or drugs to try to speed herself up? Lizzie had a good life. Why would she jeopardize it? I wander into the living room. The furniture is worn and pleasant: a mauve fabric loveseat and sofa, a couple of end tables. Everywhere I look I see photographs of Lizzie, some by herself, most in various poses with JP. I pick up the wedding photo and study it, remembering that day at City Hall: Lizzie smiling with joy in her white pantsuit, a scarlet rose corsage pinned to it, JP grinning proudly in a purple tuxedo. I was relieved that they didn't have a religious ceremony. Even though I'd come to terms with Lizzie's sexuality and knew how happy she was, the idea of enshrining her relationship in a holy ceremony would have made me uncomfortable.

The whole of one wall is covered from floor to ceiling in bookshelves. I approach and look closer. They're organized into themes. On the middle shelf are large tomes of classical literature. Above that, there are an awful lot of lurid looking novels with pictures of barely-clad women on them. The bottom shelf is where Lizzie put her religious books, everything from Christianity to Wicca. I assume most of the books are Lizzie's, since JP's always proclaimed that she's not much of a reader. Perhaps this evening I'll spend time looking through them and decide which ones I might want to take with me.

Across from the bookshelf is a smaller shelf, with Lizzie's old fuzzy rabbit, Harvella, and a set of Russian dolls my father gave her one Christmas. Behind them, barely visible, is a little knitted doll. I pounce on it. When we were children, Mom knitted two dolls, one for me and one for Lizzie. She used multicolored wool and somehow managed to get the blue parts where the eyes were and red for the mouths. After she stuffed and sewed the dolls up, she embroidered our two names intertwined on red felt hearts which she stuck on the dolls.

"Whatever happens to you both in life, you'll always have each other," she said when she gave them to us one Christmas Eve, when I was seven and Lizzie was five.

After she and Daddy died, I thought it was some kind

of premonition, as if Mom knew it would only be the two of us going through life together. The doll won't mean anything to JP, she probably thinks it's just a ratty, little piece of junk, but it will mean everything to me.

Something catches my eye. Beyond the living room is a patio that leads into the garden where JP said she was going. I look out and see that JP is sitting on her haunches in one of the flowerbeds. It almost looks as if she's praying, until she starts scrabbling at the dirt, picking it up in handfuls and throwing it around her.

I yank open the French doors and run across the patio. JP is screaming. "Why? Why?" The wind catches a fistful of dirt that boomerangs and hits her in the face. "Why did you have to...?" Is she asking God why He took Lizzie? Does she believe in something after all? Or is she asking Lizzie why she had to die?

She screams repeatedly, still throwing soil, covering herself in dirt, dead leaves swirling around her as she paws at the ground like an angry dog chained to a fence. Then she pounds the hard earth and punches it with her fists.

"We had a good life!" She gasps and heaves. Fat tears and snot mingle on her sleeve, which she rubs viciously across her face. "It could have gone on forever."

I move closer, but she doesn't even see me. She punches her forehead with knuckles that are red from pounding the earth. "It's not fair! Not fair!" She screams and scrabbles in the dirt and flails around helplessly, until she falls flat on her face, exhausted and spent.

I've never seen an outpouring of grief like this; it feels so raw and deep.

She's still lying on the ground when I approach her and whisper softly, "JP?"

"*Lizzie?*" She raises her head, her eyes wide and full of hope, until she realizes it's me and slumps back down again.

I touch her shoulder lightly. "Come on, JP, let's get you up." I talk to her, calm and soothing as if she's a five-year-old who's worn herself out with a tantrum, then lead her back into the house.

"Tea, or do you have anything stronger?" For the first time I notice the unwashed dishes in the sink.

She shakes her head. "I haven't let alcohol pass my

lips in years."

I've always wanted to ask her if she was also in Alcoholics Anonymous. I asked Lizzie once and she looked at me and grinned. "It's an anonymous program, sis. That means we don't tell anyone who's in and who's not."

"Tea's fine." JP shakes dirt out of her hair and brushes leaves off her sweater.

I want to tell JP about Lizzie's last words. Yet how can I mention the idea that someone may have poisoned her when JP's so distraught? The last thing I want is to push her over the edge. I have to find a better time. We both have a right to find out the truth.

Chapter Four

The next evening, we gather in JP's living room. Paula has put out two concentric circles of chairs and a little table in the middle covered with a blue silk shawl. The room is so full some people are standing behind the circles of chairs and others sit on the floor. The only people I know are JP and Paula; the others quickly introduce themselves.

A small, wiry, woman speaks first. "I'm Helen. We took the same Zumba class every evening at the fitness center. The first day I joined, Lizzie told me to stand next to her so I could copy her steps. The next day she said, 'If we're going to dance together, don't you think we should know each other's names?' That was Lizzie." She sighs. "Always friendly and helpful."

Everyone nods and people start to tear up.

"Doris," announces a wrinkly woman with gnarled hands and spectacular silver hair. "I'm the book goddess." Everyone laughs. "We formed a book club a few months ago. Lizzie dubbed me the book goddess because I'd read so much and had so many suggestions that they all decided I should be the one to choose the books. Lizzie was the one who invited me to the club. It didn't matter to her that I was old enough to be her grandmother, or that I needed a ride. Sometimes she took me out for lunch. She was so kind."

The next woman to speak up is a tall woman with dark skin and aquiline features. Her black braids are twisted in an updo toward the back of her head that accentuates strong cheekbones and a tight jaw. Her eyes have the kindest expression I've ever seen.

"Cleo," she says, then turns to me. "The family

resemblance is amazing."

I smile ruefully. "I know. When we were kids people used to ask us all the time, 'Are you twins?' As a child I'd respond huffily, 'I'm two years older.' Now if they ask, I'm flattered by the compliment." As soon as I say it, I remember they won't be asking, not ever again. I choke back a sob.

"We're all going to miss Lizzie so much," Cleo says, and this time I notice how deep and melodious her voice is.

"You have a beautiful voice," I blurt out, surprising myself.

"Thank you. I love to use it for singing."

"Me too. I'm a soprano in my church choir."

"I sing at church too. Alto." Her eyes sparkle at me, and a quiver runs through my body. My groin tightens and a little hollow place in my stomach feels as if it's filling up with butterflies. I tighten my grip on the arms of the chair. The feeling is familiar, and I don't want to have it. Especially not now, at Lizzie's memorial. I've promised myself. And for years I've kept my promise. Images fill my mind. Two young girls in college...

I miss the next two people to introduce themselves as I try desperately to put the past out of my mind. I force myself into the present and listen to the remainder of the introductions. People from her work, friends from various activities. There is nobody called Jim. Although, if Jim is the one who poisoned her, that's hardly surprising. Who was he? How did he do it? I want to focus on this memorial, but I also want to get to know these people so that maybe one of them can help me solve the puzzle.

Paula leans forward to light the candle on the small table in front of her and places a little pebble next to it. A musky scent fills the air, sweet and earthy.

"If any of you would like to add something to our altar and tell us about its connection to Lizzie, please do," Paula says. Her use of the word altar feels very pagan. I hope I'm not going to be too uncomfortable.

Several people come forward to put items on the table. When one of them puts a little plate with a lemon bar on it, I smile and sob at the same time.

The woman, whose name I've forgotten already, says,

"It was her favorite dessert."

"I know," I tell them. "Mom had a secret recipe for it. I always bake it for special occasions."

"So did Lizzie," the woman says, and everyone sighs. Someone places a small blue book on the table, which I'm pretty sure is a miniature version of the AA big book. Someone else puts a pale-white sand dollar down, along with a round silver coin.

"She loved Atlantic City—the beach and the casino."

I admit to being slightly shocked that Lizzie would gamble, but after all, her life changed a lot when she moved east.

Ben, a middle-aged man, puts out a name badge with the public library logo on it. "She was the best colleague a person could ever want. I don't know how I'll manage at work without her."

Doris gets up and turns to Paula. "Can you help me with something, dear?" They leave the room, and when they return, Paula is staggering under the weight of a dozen or so books.

"I couldn't decide which one to put on the altar. These are the books we read in the last year. Lizzie had something profound to say about every one of them."

Paula turns to JP and me. "Would you like to add anything?"

JP shakes her head. "If I could rip out my heart and break it into pieces..."

There's an awkward silence.

"Lizzie loved you so much. And in turn, you were there for her," Paula says. "You were a fun couple, and after she got her diagnosis, you took excellent care of her. She was lucky to have such a committed partner."

Several people nod their heads in agreement.

"No!" JP's face turns red. "Don't. I wasn't a good wife to her. I got mad at her..."

"Of course you did," Cleo says. "Who doesn't get upset with their partner sometimes? You two were good together." I wonder if she has a partner. I didn't notice her arrive with anyone.

"Lizzie was lucky. As well as JP, she had her loving sister." Paula turns to face me. "She always spoke well of you, even though there were ways in which the two of you

didn't see eye to eye. That's the best kind of relationship—
when you can agree to disagree."
"Thanks," I say. "She certainly moved away from the
life we were brought up to. I had to do a lot of growing to
accept her new lifestyle."
"But you succeeded. She was always so scared that you
might pull away from her."
"Lizzie was all I had." I choke back a sob and Cleo
moves over to put her arm around me. I want to fold
myself into her, but instead I pull back.
"I have something to put on the table," I say. I pull the
knitted doll out of my purse. "Lizzie and I were orphaned
when I was 19 and she was 17. Many years before that,
Mom made these dolls for us. Lizzie once said to me,
'Sometimes I think about when we're both old ladies and
can't remember too much of anything. When I put this on
my mantelpiece in the nursing home, even if I don't
remember who made it and who has the other one, I'll
know it represents unending love.'" I barely get the words
out before I start crying again.
Paula turns to JP. "Would you like to say some words
about Lizzie? Tell us a little about what made her special."
JP looks bewildered and her voice is gruff. "I'm not
one for speaking, and you all know what made her
unique."
"Is there something you'd say to her, right now, if you
could?" Paula asks. "Just a sentence. Anything you want."
JP hesitates. She looks around her and then stares into
a far-off place. "How could you make my life so perfect—
and then ruin it?" The moment the words are out of her
mouth, she starts to howl and pull at her hair. Paula rushes
over to her.
"You're okay, JP," she says in a soothing voice,
stroking JP's hair. "We're all here to support you. You have
no need to fear. We're with you today and we'll be with you
on the   journey ahead."
JP looks around, her eyes unfocused, as if she's unsure
where she is, but her keening subsides and she sits down,
her arms limp at her side.
"Life is precious," Paula says, "and its loss can feel
unbearable. Together we can move forward, remembering
Lizzie, honoring the amazing person she was." She pulls

out a piece of paper and starts reading from it.

"Don't think of me beneath the earth.
Think of me when the earth gives life to spring's
first flowers,
When summer rain fills the air with the rich, sweet
scent of earth and grass, leaf and tree."

I glance at JP, remembering how she was scrabbling in the earth today. Does this resonate with her? I lean over and squeeze her hand but she pulls it away. Even though this   service is nothing like the one I'd hoped to have, I can't help feeling grateful that Lizzie found this community of women who obviously loved and cared about her so much. Doris reads a verse then passes the paper to Helen.

"When you gaze up at the starlit heavens,
Remember, the light once mine still shines within you.
Think of me, remember me, and my light will shine on
through you."

It's beautiful. There is silence, except for the soft crying of several women.

Then Cleo stands up, and begins singing, her voice strong and powerful. *"Amazing Grace, how sweet the sound..."*

The haunting melody with its praise of God is the exact song I would have wanted had I planned this ritual, and Cleo's voice accentuates all the beauty and sadness I've ever felt. I feel the spirit within me move and go over to stand by her side.

"Twas grace that taught my heart to fear..." I sing in harmony with Cleo, lifting my words so that they fly upward to heaven. Cleo turns and faces me and together we sing, *"I once was lost..."*

When we finish, the room is completely hushed. I had intended to read Psalm 23, The Lord is my Shepherd, and to ask people to say the Lord's Prayer with me. Would it be right to do a memorial without these prayers? I look around the room and feel within my heart that this moment is perfect, and it will suffice.

After the ritual is over, everyone moves into the dining room where they've filled the table with homemade casseroles, sandwiches, cakes and pastries. They talk to each other in small groups. I nibble on some celery and wonder who I can ask about Jim, or how I can find out if anyone knows about Lizzie's affair.

Helen is standing to one side so I go over and start chatting. After a few moments of small talk I ask, "Do you know a friend of Lizzie's called Jim?"

She shakes her head. "No. But our classes were all female, so I wouldn't be likely to. Why don't you ask Janelle?" She points me toward the sole woman who seems to have dressed the way I might have expected someone at a funeral to dress: black dress and black pumps. Most of the attendees are wearing sweaters and jeans, and only a couple are in black. I approach her and hold out my hand.

"Thanks for coming tonight," I say.

"I'm glad Paula invited me. Lizzie saved my life."

I feel proud, though I can't quite picture Lizzie diving into a lake or performing mouth-to-mouth. "What did she do?"

"She saved me from the clutches of alcohol. She was my sponsor for years, until she quit the program."

"She quit? You mean she started drinking?"

Janelle looks shocked. "Oh no. I mean, I couldn't say for sure since I haven't seen her in over a year. She decided she was very solid in her sobriety and that she wanted to focus on other things. Sometimes it was hard for her to be surrounded by a bunch of drunks. It made her think more about drinking than she would otherwise."

"I hope she didn't really refer to you as a bunch of drunks," I say, and she smiles. "Do you happen to know someone called Jim? Did she by any chance have a sponsee by that name?"

She shakes her head. "Not a sponsee, but her sponsor was a lovely guy called Jimmy, if that's who you mean."

My heart skips a beat. I can't believe I found him so quickly. "Yes, Jimmy. He's not here tonight. Did they have a falling out?"

"Not as far as I know. She always spoke about him with the utmost respect. I don't know if they kept in touch after she stopped coming to the rooms."

"The rooms?"

"It's what we call our meetings, the rooms of AA, or just the rooms, for short."

"I know it's an anonymous program, but I really need to contact him. Can you tell me where I could find him?"

She cocks her head to one side and pauses. "I have no idea what his last name is, and I haven't seen him for quite a while. I'm sure I'd have heard if he went out—started drinking or something. Perhaps he moved away. Sorry, I can't help you with that."

Janelle moves over to the table to fix herself a plate of food and I do likewise. I'm disappointed that I didn't get all the information I need; however, I'm more than satisfied by the fact that I already know who Jim is.

Now I just have to track him down.

Chapter Five

"Is there anything else of Lizzie's you want?" JP asks as I force myself to eat a bowl of cereal before she takes me to the airport. I've already taken a threadbare sweater Mom knitted, which Lizzie had kept all these years; the well-worn bible she received when she was baptized, which she obviously couldn't bring herself to let go; and of course, my doll. There's a box of books JP is going to send by mail.

"I was wondering about some family heirlooms... jewelry..."

"Of course. I kept meaning to have you look through that stuff." JP leaves the room and I hear her run upstairs.

After Mom died, Lizzie and I divided up the small amount of jewelry she had. I got Mom's wedding ring and a sapphire pin, and Lizzie took Mom's emerald engagement ring and an emerald bracelet that was my grandmother's. JP returns a few moments later and hands me a large three-tiered wooden box. There are a variety of rings, bracelets and necklaces, most of them cheap, gaudy things, brightly colored with many in the form of rainbows. I don't see emeralds of any kind. Indeed, there's nothing semiprecious or precious at all. I try to remember if I ever saw Lizzie wearing the gemstones, but the only thing I can picture was her gold wedding band, a simple ring that JP told me they had to cut off her after she got so bloated.

"Do you know what happened to the ring and bracelet that were my grandmother's and my mom's?"

JP shakes her head.

"They were emeralds. Not necessarily valuable, but...sentimental."

"I wouldn't know an emerald from a ruby," she says. "I

never saw Lizzie wear anything like that though."

Where could they be? Did she keep them somewhere hidden? Did she have other jewelry—gifts from the mystery lover—she didn't want JP to see?

As we drive to the airport, I can't help but remember the first time I met JP at this same airport.

It was the summer after Lizzie moved to Philadelphia to get away from Kurt. It had been almost a year since she'd moved, and I was excited to see her. While I was waiting to board my plane, a text came in saying Lizzie's car had broken down so her new best friend, JP, would meet me. "Look for a deep-blue pickup truck," the text read.

The moment I stepped out of the airport terminal, the fetid, muggy, ninety-degree air of a Philly day in August assaulted me. I spotted the truck right away and noted the tall figure leaning against the passenger door, dark hair barely visible beneath a baseball cap. Despite the excessive heat, JP was sporting jeans and black, steel-tipped Doc Martens. I wiped the sweat off my forehead and maneuvered myself and my oversized luggage toward the truck.

"You must be JP," I said, smiling politely, since I had no free hand to extend for a handshake.

JP nodded and took my suitcase from me. "Nice to finally meet my girlfriend's sister. Lizzie talks about you all the time."

"Oh that sly thing! Lizzie said you were her best friend. She didn't tell me she had a boyfriend."

There was a moment of absolute silence. Then JP said stonily, "She doesn't. I'm a woman."

I was embarrassed and confused all at the same time. I'd never met a woman who looked or dressed anything like JP. Why would a woman choose to look like a man? And what did it mean that Lizzie was her girlfriend?

I apologized profusely. JP shrugged.

"Let's go," she said and drove to their home, mostly in silence. I felt horrified. My sister's best friend, and I'd made a colossal faux pas. Once I got to know JP better, I would learn that social skills weren't her strong suit, but at the time I thought she was freezing me out.

I felt mortified but also thoroughly confused. There

were so many levels on which none of this made sense. Lizzie was a devout Christian. We'd both grown up in the church and loved everything about it. Lizzie taught Sunday school and helped out with the youth ministry. The highlights of my week had always been, and still were, choir rehearsal on Wednesday evening and singing at Sunday services. Lizzie had taken a chastity pledge, which had been part of the reason she'd been so anxious to marry Kurt once she started dating him. How could she of all people now be dating a woman? Our whole lives we'd been told that there was only one right form of sexuality and being with a woman clearly wasn't it. Was she going through a phase? She'd just come out of a bad marriage. Was this some sort of unusual rebound?

Later that evening, while JP was in the kitchen preparing dinner, I cornered Lizzie.

"Is she really your girlfriend?"

She nodded.

"Why didn't you tell me?"

"I wanted to wait and tell you in person. So you could see what an amazing person JP is before you rushed to any kind of judgment."

"It's not up to me to judge you. But aren't you afraid that you will be judged by our Heavenly Father?"

Lizzie shook her head. "No. I've given all that up. Once I got to know JP and all my new friends, they showed me how Christianity is misogynous and sexist. It's just a tool of   patriarchy, intent on putting women down."

"That's not true! You've always been happy in the church, and so have I. We have a very important role to play—"

"Exactly! The church makes us play roles, like wife and mother. That's what I was trying to do when I married Kurt. I'm done playing roles."

After a year of not having seen her, I didn't want to argue with my beloved sister. But I had one question I couldn't leave unasked.

"I didn't mean to upset JP and I certainly didn't want to hurt her feelings, but I can't be the only one who's mistaken her for a man. Why does she dress that way?"

Lizzie sighed. "For goodness sake, Ash."

"What?"

"JP hates being mistaken for a man. Why did you do that. Because she has short hair?"

I shook my head. Lizzie knew I'd never met anyone like JP before, but she remained defensive about it. At first I thought JP was mad at me because she was so quiet when I was around, but when a couple of their friends came over, I could see that she was quiet with them too. The strong, silent type, I said to myself, and over the years that impression remained with me.

That first visit I felt as if Lizzie was pushing me to accept ideas and practices instantly, just because she had.

"How do you reconcile your new lifestyle with everything we've been taught about it being wrong and sinful?" I asked her.

She sighed again. "I don't care what we've been taught. It's all lies. I don't need to reconcile it."

"But I do. I'm still a woman of faith and I can't just switch it off. When Mom and Dad died, I don't know what I'd have done if the church and our church friends weren't there for me. When I'm feeling down, my faith lifts me up. I feel more at peace and in touch with my soul in church than in any other place. Even when I'm not in church, I can say a prayer or sing a hymn and bring myself to a better place. Don't you feel that way anymore?"

"I feel that way when I'm wrapped in JP's arms."

Was she purposely being provocative?

"Aren't you scared God will punish you?"

Lizzie looked at me impatiently. "Look around you Ash, there are millions of people in this world going unpunished."

"What about your spiritual wellbeing? Aren't you scared you're damning yourself for eternity?"

"Oh for Pete's sake. Don't tell me you still believe that? I'm the younger of the two of us, but you need to grow up. That's just stuff they tell us when we're kids, to get us to believe."

It wasn't of course. Millions of people all over the world held the same beliefs I did, and we couldn't all be wrong.

"Can't you be happy for me?" Lizzie wanted my approval so badly, and I wanted to support her.

"I'm glad you feel happy," I told her, torn between her

needs and my beliefs. "Give me some time to work through my own stuff."

She did, and gradually we returned to our old closeness.

I can't say that JP and I were close in the same way. JP has an outer shell that's hard to crack. She has always been completely dedicated to Lizzie, and for that I love her. And I believe she loves me for the same reason. But it's one thing to care about someone, and another to be able to have a good conversation with them. Up until now I never had to interact with JP without Lizzie as a buffer, but now it's just her and me. Both grieving, both feeling lost.

"We'll stay in touch?" I ask, half questioning, half stating, as I pull my suitcase out of the pickup.

"Sure. Don't expect daily calls. You know it's not my style." She grimaces, acknowledging her lack of social finesse, and I smile back. I put down the suitcase and give her a hug.

"We're family, JP. We have to be there for each other. It's what Lizzie would want." She nods, wordlessly, both of us tearing up at the mention of our beloved girl.

I drag myself through the terminal doors. At the memorial I felt such a sense of connection with Lizzie through her friends. Now, walking toward security, all I feel is a sense of isolation. I try to tell myself I still have JP, but the feeling of desolation only increases.

Chapter Six

When I return to work the following day, my colleagues gather round to offer their condolences. I work at a highly regarded, private, Christian middle school doing everything from fundraising to leading the choir, and sometimes my workplace feels more like home than my apartment does.

"Are you sure you should be back at work already?" Luke, the principal, gives me a hug as soon as I walk into the teachers' lounge.

I nod. "No point in staying home and feeling sorry for myself."

Luke hands me a large white envelope decorated with doves. When I open it there's a card inside with a beautiful message reminding me that Lizzie is in a better place. It's been signed by all the administrators, faculty and staff.

"We were wondering if you'd like to have some sort of memorial service? We'd like to help you give your sister a good send-off to heaven, and maybe you can share some of your memories of her with us."

It's exactly what I need. We spend a few minutes discussing which hymns and readings to use, and then I get ready to head to my office.

"By the way, on Friday we had a staff meeting where everyone signed a new form our legal department came up with. I've put it in your box. Ask me if you have any questions about it. Otherwise if you can just sign it and pass it on to HR, that would be great."

I've only been gone a few days, and already the work has piled up. I left in such a hurry I forgot to put an away message on my voicemail, so I have a couple of calls from folks wondering why I'm not getting back to them. Two messages are from the choir mistress of a gospel band I'm trying to get for our fall fundraiser and another is from a nonprofit asking if we'll co-sponsor an event they're putting on. I wasn't sure whether I'd be able to focus on my job so soon after Lizzie's death, but before I know it, the whole morning has passed and Luke is sticking his head around my door.

"Want to do lunch?"

I've only had lunch with him twice since I started here, so it's nice to feel he's looking out for me. I push aside my papers and gather up my purse.

"Did you sign that form yet?" he asks as I stand up.

"I glanced at it when I went through my mail but didn't have a chance to peruse the details." I pull it out from under a stack of papers and take a quick look.

"It's the new Statement of Faith all our staff are required to sign, the one you signed when you first took the job. No major changes. We added in a clause stating that if we counsel any of the children, we'll follow the ethics code of the American Association of Christian Counselors."

"Even if we're not professional therapists?"

"All of us talk to the kids and help them with their dilemmas. We thought this was a good way of ensuring we're all on the same page. It's nothing you would have a problem with."

"I'm sure it isn't. Sounds like a great organization. I'll read through it after lunch and sign it, I promise."

We head out to Luke's car, and as we drive, I sit back and revel in the scenery. It's why I've always loved living in the Sierra foothills. At Lizzie's, the trees were still bare, the air cold and uninviting. Here the hills have turned green and the first wildflowers are starting to appear. The majestic snowcapped mountains lend majesty to the scenery.

After lunch I switch from fundraising to music lessons. Our music teacher is on maternity leave, so in addition to running choir practice, I'm also doing some individual piano and violin tutoring. The first student is a girl I can see has done zero practice since the last lesson. I don't understand why kids think I won't know when it's so obvious.

"Do you like playing the piano?" I try to keep the impatience out of my voice.

"It's okay. I really wanted to play the saxophone, but Mom says since we already have a piano in the house, that's what I have to learn."

There's nothing worse than teaching a child who has no interest in learning.

"Why the saxophone?"

"I like jazz. I know kids my age aren't meant to, but I think it's cool."

I have an idea. I move over a little on the piano bench we're sharing and start playing a few bars of a piece.

Anna's eyes light up. "That's great. What is it?"

"Scott Joplin. Would you like to learn it?"

The rest of the lesson, Anna stays completely involved. I have a feeling she'll be practicing plenty this week.

When I return to the office, I barely have the chance to respond to some pressing emails before it's time to leave. Tonight is choir practice, so I never work late on a Wednesday. Then I remember the form Luke wanted me to sign. I pick it up and start reading. It's interesting. Talks about how we use our beliefs as an ethical foundation for working with people. It seems to reflect everything I believe: that the Bible is the inspired Word of God and therefore "the preeminent model for Christian counseling practice...and the final authority for all matters about which it speaks." I glance through the foundations: counseling involves a "dedicated relationship with the worldwide church...a Spirit-led process of change, transformation, and growth...respect for everyone." There's more, but as Luke said, it's nothing I don't believe in, so I sign the form and put it in the HR inbox on my way out the door.

Driving home, I reflect on how Lizzie lost her faith. As far as I could tell it was purely because she fell in love with JP and she wasn't willing to forgo that love. All that other stuff about patriarchy and sexism came later. I tried to explain that turning away from God and living the way she was wouldn't come without a price. I never shared my own experience with her because I couldn't bear the blame that would undoubtedly follow once she knew the truth. I tried to warn her. When that didn't work, I reminded her that she shouldn't judge all men by Kurt. She said that now she was with JP she truly understood what real passion was, and how true love felt.

"You just haven't met the right man," I told her and she groaned so loudly I thought she was ill.

"No," she said, "*you* just haven't met the right man." She was right about that. Dating has always been hard for me. Maybe I'm a perfectionist, but it's so easy to find fault with potential mates. When Lizzie was married to Kurt, she persuaded me to sign up for a Christian online matchmaking website. I got a ton of hits on my profile and went out with several of the men. The first one almost put me off dating for good: even though I told him I was a virgin, he kept asking questions about my past sex life. Lizzie said not to worry about it and encouraged me to try again. The second guy was nice and we went out several times. He was a financial advisor, quiet, with a dry sense of humor. He was thrilled to know I'd been keeping myself for a future husband, even though I didn't like to tell him I'd never met anyone I was tempted to go all the way with. After four dates, he asked me to marry him. I asked him how he was so sure he loved me.

"I don't know if I love you or not. Through our joint love of Christ, I believe we could come to love each other. Surely all that matters is that we're both virgins, and we're both   serious about wanting to build a family and devote ourselves to the Lord?"

I knew he was right, but it sounded like an arranged marriage from another religion and I didn't want that. I still don't. Even though it hasn't happened yet, I'm only thirty-five and I haven't given up hope.

Chapter Seven

I've been home for over a month and still done nothing about tracking down Lizzie's former sponsor, and possible lover, Jimmy. I ruminate on it at night when I can't sleep, but in the morning I tell myself it's ridiculous, that there's no way my sister was part of some sinister murder. I try to put it out of my mind, but nothing works. Eventually I decide to give JP a call. Perhaps I'll tell her what Lizzie said and see what she thinks. Or at least find out what she knew about Jim because it sounded as if JP did know about the affair. But Lizzie said JP was mad about it, so I'll have to be careful how I bring it up and what I say.

Since returning home, I've spoken to JP a couple of times. Our conversations are awkward; they stutter along then peter out. I can see it's going to be a struggle to keep our relationship going, but for Lizzie's sake I want to try.

The phone goes to voicemail. Is JP avoiding my calls? It wouldn't surprise me. But it's the only way I can contact her. She doesn't use Facebook or email because she's on the computer all day for her job and said she can't wait to get off it once she's done with work.

I wish I had someone to confide in about what Lizzie said. Was she just delirious? The idea that someone would have poisoned her is insane, and yet it's also crazy that she died from an illness that should have been perfectly manageable. JP said that drinking when you have FSGS was enough to kill Lizzie, but that almost makes it sound as if my sister had a death wish. I refuse to believe that.

I have to confide in someone, so when I can't get through to JP, I decide it's time to see a therapist. I consider going through the church, but sometimes our world is too small for comfort so I call my Employee

Assistance Program. They're happy to provide me with a list of five names. I pick one at random and am able to set an appointment for the next day.

Dr. Lim's office is in a nondescript two-story office building in the commercial center. The outside of the building may be plain but the waiting room is the total opposite. Embroidered tapestries adorn the walls. One tapestry has an image of two fish jumping out of the water, another has a yellow lotus flower, a third has a picture of a wheel. They look as if they're from some exotic country like Thailand or India. Little statues of Buddha sit together on the nesting tables, and I have a sudden stab of anxiety wondering whether I should have asked for a Christian counselor after all. Based on the waiting room decor, I picture Dr. Lim as a willowy ethereal woman wearing a flowing Indian print skirt, with her long dark hair in a braid down her back. When the door opens, I'm greeted by a plump woman in a maroon suit who offers me a cup of hazelnut coffee.

"Tell me what brings you here," she says after I'm seated on a comfortable leather sofa. "I don't need any background yet, just tell me what made you pick up the phone and call."

"My sister died recently," I say. Dr. Lim raises her eyebrows in surprise. Women my age aren't meant to have sisters die on them. An elderly parent maybe, a grandparent even, but not their thirty-three-year-old sister.

I describe rushing to Philly and my all-too-brief interaction with Lizzie before she died. I tell Dr. Lim what I think Lizzie said, but that I can't be sure. She listens without interrupting.

"You're so sad about your sister," she says finally. "It's such a terrible loss for you." Even though I want to hear what she thinks about Lizzie's last words, what she says is so exactly right that I burst into tears. She doesn't try to get me to stop, as most of my school colleagues have done these past weeks when they think I may be about to cry.

"Let it all out, my dear. You are devastated. In my culture, we wail. You can wail too. It's very freeing." I'm sure she's right, but there's no way I could do that. I smile a little at the thought.

"Tell me how you've mourned your sister so far," Dr. Lim says.

I tell her about the ritual Paula did in Philadelphia and

about the memorial my colleagues put together, both so different yet equally moving.

"And what rituals do you plan to do now, to keep her present in your thoughts?" she asks.

"I—I don't know. I thought it might be time to stop thinking about her. Maybe my way of moving on is to try to solve this issue of whether someone poisoned her."

"It's too soon to let go, or to divert your attention from your grief. Americans always want to rush through the stages of grieving, but other cultures manage loss a little better. The Jewish mourning process for example is so prescribed: intense mourning for a week, then a month of restrictions, and a whole year saying a daily prayer to remember the individual who died."

"Paula's Jewish and I don't think she would have done all that," I mutter. I feel as if I'm being criticized.

Dr. Lim ignores my comment. "In Buddhism we have weekly prayers for forty-nine days. Our rituals aren't just about helping us deal with our grief. They're also to help the deceased during the post-death transformation. What do you think you need more—help for yourself to deepen your faith, or help for your sister to make her transition?"

"I don't know what you mean by transition. I know my sister is already in her heavenly home with God. I'm not sad for her, but I do want justice for her, if it hasn't been served."

"I know you believe that your sister is in a much better place, that she's gone to meet her maker. I understand you should be happy for her. But that's a tall order when you feel her loss so acutely. Do you think you're focusing on this idea of her being poisoned so you don't have to deal with your anger at God for taking her away from you? If I were you, I wouldn't just be sad, I'd be angry, hurt, confused—and lost. Where are your parents? What terrible thing happened in your family that you don't have them by your side through all this?"

"My parents died in a car crash when I was nineteen and Lizzie seventeen."

"Oh my goodness!" Dr. Lim cups her face in her hands in shock. "How awful for you. Not only did your sister die before her time, but this death must be triggering all the old feelings about how your parents died. You poor thing." She leans forward and clasps my hands in hers. I feel her warmth and sympathy. She wasn't criticizing me before; she was just trying to remind me that we all grieve in different ways.

"I know you want to know who this Jimmy might be, and what may or may not have happened to your sister, but that's not going to change anything. I believe you're focusing on that as a way not to focus on the terrible   tragedies that have befallen your family. In some ways, I don't blame you. Grief can be overwhelming. But the reason you need to let go of the whole Jimmy idea, at least for now, is that when we're in a state of grief, we can't think straight. I always encourage my patients not to make any drastic decisions or life changes while they're mourning. I believe you need to give yourself over to the day-to-day routine, allow yourself to handle your grief, and when it starts to subside, that's when you can investigate what happened to your sister, if anything did. It won't make a difference if you do it now or in six months."

"Just let it go? For six months? But what if he does it again?"

Dr. Lim looks at me with sympathy. "I've had several clients who had spouses or siblings die unexpectedly, and they all want someone to blame. Often they blame God, but since you're a Christian, that's not an option for you. So you may be trying to displace the blame by putting it on Jimmy. Perhaps your sister was also trying to place the blame for her death somewhere too. Maybe she did have an affair and the guilt was poisoning her mind. Your sister may have realized she was dying and not have been willing to accept it, just as you are unwilling to accept it. Death happens. To the young and the old, to people we expect to die and to those we don't."

I hang my head and look at the floor. In some ways what she's saying makes a lot of sense.

"Let yourself grieve, and if you still feel this way in a few months, you'll be in a much stronger place emotionally to investigate." I look up at her and nod. "Meanwhile, let's come up with some daily rituals. Could you read a poem every night? Or sing her a hymn each morning?"

By the end of the session I have a list of ideas, and when I leave her office my heart feels lighter.

Until I get home and listen to the message on my voicemail.

Chapter Eight

The voicemail is from Janelle. "I bumped into Jimmy yesterday. He was really upset when I told him about Lizzie. I have his phone number, if you want it. He said he'd be fine with you calling him."

Is the timing fate? Just when I'd decided to let go of the whole Jimmy thing?

According to this phone message, he didn't know about Lizzie. Could that be true? If he was her sponsor, even if she was no longer in AA, surely they'd have kept in touch as friends? Unless they had a falling out. Was it about the affair? Did she end it and stop all contact?

There's another possibility too: that he's pretending he didn't know about Lizzie's death, when in fact he was the one who caused it.

I call Janelle and after exchanging pleasantries, she gives me Jimmy's number.

I'm about to punch the number into my phone, when Dr. Lim's voice starts playing in my head. *You're displacing your grief. People who are grieving can't think straight.* It's important that I handle this call right. I don't want to alienate the most important person I need to talk to. I feel as if I would say the right things, but what if I wouldn't? And if I am going to talk to Jimmy, it would probably be better face-to-face, not by telephone where I can't see his expression or his body language.

I almost jump out of my skin when the phone, which I'm still holding in my hand, starts ringing. The caller ID shows it's Mike, our choirmaster at church. Mike's a gruff kind of man, so hard and demanding on new choristers that many of them drop out after the first choir practice. But once he has your back, he'll do anything for you.

"Two things," he says, bypassing any chitchat.

"Go on," I say, half-listening and half wondering what to do about Jimmy.

"There's a big alto solo in the new oratorio we're singing at our next concert. It will take a lot of extra time to study it and get it right, but it's yours if you want it. Do you?"

I've been second alto in the choir for years, and this is the first time he's offered me a major solo. The timing isn't great, what with school and figuring out what happened to Lizzie, but I don't want to miss the opportunity.

"Yes! Thank you I—" But he's already on to the second thing.

"Harriet Tubman High is performing *Fiddler on the Roof* this weekend. I have tickets for Friday evening. You want to come with me?"

I'm taken aback. Mike and I have never socialized. The first choir practice after Lizzie died, he was much more solicitous than I might have expected, but we haven't talked since then. I'm not interested in going to Tubman High, though. I have to attend all the performances at my own school, and sometimes it's hard to be enthusiastic when kids overdramatize and sing off key.

"No. Thanks anyway. Take someone who'll appreciate it more than I would," I tell him, still a little distracted. He hangs up abruptly. Is he offended? It occurs to me that perhaps he was asking me on a date, but I quickly dispel that idea; no one in their right mind would invite someone to a high school performance for a romantic interlude. Plus, Mike doesn't date, we all know that. I put it out of my mind and turn back to what was occupying my thoughts before he called.

Maybe instead of pursuing Jimmy, I should find out more about Lizzie's medical condition and how serious it really was.

I sit at the kitchen table and rack my brains. I try to remember exactly what Lizzie told me that day she called me after she got the diagnosis, about a year before she died.

෮ම

It was a cold winter's day, and I'd built a log fire to keep warm. After the shock of her disclosure, I asked her to explain it in a little more detail.

"Focal Segmental Glomerulosclerosis. It's basically scarred kidneys. It's fairly rare and they don't know why I have it. It could be the result of an infection or drug toxicity, and they're trying to rule out possible causes like diabetes, lupus or HIV."

"Jeez." I breathed softly. "HIV? From Kurt?"

"Highly unlikely. I should have the test results this week. But they said there may be a genetic component too."

I fell silent. A genetic component? Mom and Dad were completely healthy when they died, as far as I knew. And then it hit me. She meant me. That I could have it too.

"What are the symptoms?" My voice was shaky.

"Too much protein in my urine, not enough in my blood. Some of them I've had for years, like high cholesterol and high blood pressure, but Dr. Marshall didn't pick up on them being related to any kind of disorder. I thought I was just getting older."

"Can they cure it?" I was pretty sure I knew the answer, but I needed to hear her say it.

"No. They said it'll keep progressing, and eventually I might need a kidney transplant or dialysis. They think that would be years down the road, if it ever even gets to that point."

"Oh, sis, I'm so sorry. What can I do?"

"Get yourself tested."

"I will. My cholesterol's always been fine, and so has my blood pressure, so I should be OK. And hopefully you will be too."

After I got off the phone I researched everything I could find about FSGS. It was pretty much what she'd told me. People could have different levels of severity, and it could develop into something more serious or not. I read that there were some dietary changes she could make, and how important it was not to do drugs or alcohol. I called her back to ask her about that. I got JP.

"Lizzie's not here. What did you want?" She always sounded like a drill sergeant on the phone, at least when she talked to me.

"I—I just wondered if the doctor had talked to Lizzie about her diet?"

"Yes he did." She sounded abrupt, but then she softened a little, "I know you're worried about her, but we're going to take good care to ensure this thing never develops into anything serious. Okay?"

෴

Only eleven months later, Lizzie was admitted to the Emergency Room the first time. Her protein levels had shot through the roof as had her potassium. They couldn't understand what had caused it, but they assured her they'd have it under control with steroids. I spoke to her after they released her, and she promised me she was already feeling better. I should have flown down then, but I had no idea how quickly things would deteriorate. We spoke on the phone a couple of times over the next few weeks, and then all of a sudden she was back in the ER, and this time she never left it.

JP and everyone at the hospital assured me that it was quite possible that going on a drinking binge was enough to shut down Lizzie's kidneys. But what if it wasn't? What if Lizzie was out drinking with Jimmy and he put something in her drink? What if they both dropped out of AA at the same time and started drinking? And what if Lizzie was trying to get him to stop?

My brain feels as if it will burst right out of my head. I have so many questions. If Jimmy did something wrong, for sure he'll be wary of talking to me, even though Janelle said he was open to it.

Dr. Lim's right about one thing: I can't think straight. I'm going to have to let all this settle a little, until I can figure out just how to get to the bottom of it.

Chapter Nine

I'm at work when my cell phone shows I missed a call from Paula. I wait until the lunch hour before calling her back.

"I've been thinking about Lizzie so much. She and JP came to us every year for our Memorial Day picnic, along with some of the folks you met at the memorial. Would you like to join us and be with people who considered Lizzie family?"

I feel a warm glow of gratitude. It could be good to spend time with Lizzie's friends and with JP. It could also be the perfect opportunity to try to find Jimmy and meet with him in person.

"I'd love to."

"You can stay with me and Beth," Paula says.

"If JP will have me, I'll stay with her. I haven't had much success connecting with her over the phone."

"Good idea. JP's been keeping her distance from everyone." There's a note of frustration in Paula's voice.

I glance at my watch. "I have to go. It's time for me to lead choir practice."

&❧

The practice room stinks of cologne and perfume. I've tried to ask that at least on practice days they tone it down, but they're all trying so hard to be cool, I haven't made much of an impact. I walk them through their voice warm-ups and their scales. It's always hard to get kids to settle down when there's a holiday in the air and especially now that we're so close to the end of the year.

"What are your plans for Memorial Day?" I ask when

we take a break between songs.

"I hate Memorial Day." The speaker is Jordan, a fourteen-year-old multitalented student, who's a gifted musician but is determined to get to college on an athletics scholarship.

"I know it's painful for those who've lost family in Iraq or Afghanistan. Did you?" I try to look as sympathetic as I can.

Jordan seems abashed. "I wasn't thinking about that. In our family it's just a big excuse for a barbecue."

"In that case, what's to hate?"

"I can't stand the smell of all that meat. It makes me sick. But my dad refuses to let me be a vegetarian. He says it's a slap in the face to God who provided us dominion over the animals."

"Boy, that's tough. But why do you hate the whole holiday?"

"It makes me feel fat and lazy. It's just one long day of eating and watching TV. When I tell my dad I want to go for a run or practice my cello, he says it's a family day and I don't need to work out or practice."

"He has a point doesn't he?"

"No." This time it's one of the girls who answers. I've been a bit concerned that she's getting rather skinny, but she's at that age where some of the kids lose their baby fat and start to look more like adults. "A regimen is a regimen and you can't take breaks whenever you feel like it." She pouts like a child. "I can't believe you of all people would agree with him." Fourteen is such an awkward age. They try so hard to sound mature, but sometimes they still act like little kids.

"One day off won't kill any of you," I reply. "Memorial Day is a time to feel grateful that we have families to spend time with." My eyes fill with tears and I turn away.

After we put away the music stands, Jordan hangs back.

"What is it?"

"It's just that, well...I find that if I don't do things exactly the same, it's too easy to slip into bad habits. Like not saying my prayers. When I was at my cousin's for a few days, he didn't pray at night, so I didn't either. When I got home, I couldn't get back into it again. I always used to ask our Lord to keep everyone safe, but then He did, even without me asking. I'm scared that if I don't run every day, I might not want to keep going."

"You have to do it because you love it, not for the rewards. We don't pray just to have good things happen to us. We pray to constantly remind ourselves of our connection to God. If one day of running would put you off doing it again, why do it?"

Jordan's eyes fill with alarm. "You know why. I can't get into college any other way."

"Yes, but I thought you loved running."

He shrugs. "I don't hate it. But I'd give it up tomorrow if I thought I could get into any good school without it."

"It seems to me that as long as you remind yourself of why you're doing it, then even if you take a break for a day or two, it'll be easy enough to get back on track."

Jordan nods. "You're right. Thanks, Miss Glynn. I'll think of you next time I drag my sorry ass out of bed first thing in the morning." He grins and runs off.

I love working with these kids. They give me a sense of accomplishment. Most of their problems are pretty simple, and I enjoy helping them solve them.

If only mine were equally easy.

Ever since that phone call from Paula, I've been stuck on something she said at the end of the call.

"Cleo seemed very excited when she heard I was inviting you. I'll have to ensure you two have time together."

It was almost enough to put me off going. The last thing I need is to be dealing with long-ago feelings that I've tucked far away and out of sight. I'm a Christian. And while Lizzie might not have been strong enough in her faith to believe she had to withstand temptation, I am.

At least I think I am.

Chapter Ten

"Don't tell me how much weight I've gained," JP says when she picks me up at the airport. "I know it already."

"You were all skin and bones when I saw you last, so it's probably not a bad thing. Are you taking care of yourself?"

"I don't need to. Everyone else takes care of me. You have no idea how many casseroles and cakes an army of lesbians can bake."

I watch the city come into view and try not to dwell on the last time she drove me from the airport. It's hard not to relive it. She's quiet too and I suspect we're both thinking the same thoughts.

🍂

"How are you doing, really?" I ask JP later that evening as we sit at the kitchen table drinking hot cups of strong chai tea.

"I'm doing better than I was. Lizzie always said that the best thing about my profession was that I could go to work in my pajamas. She was right—for weeks I barely got dressed."

"Have you been able to go out and start socializing?"

"The gang's been trying to get me out of the house, but I can't bear to mix with people who knew and loved Lizzie. When I'm with them, I feel her absence more than ever. I've never needed to be around people. As long as I had Lizzie everyone else was just kinda background noise."

"But now that she's not around, don't you need that background noise? Isn't it awfully quiet otherwise?"

"Don't get me wrong. They're all nice enough—Paula,

Cleo, Doris and that whole gang—but I don't have any energy to give them. Paula always says, 'you don't have to entertain us, honey, just let us be there for you.' I don't want to look mean or callous, but she doesn't understand that she can't be there for me. Nobody can."

"But something's happened. You're doing much better. I can see that." Not only has JP filled out, but she's cleaned the house and got rid of a lot of clutter. She and Lizzie were never much for housekeeping, and in all the houses they lived, I always felt like I had to be careful not to trip on slippers or boxes or the vacuum cleaner. I used to tell Lizzie that's what closets were for, but she'd just laugh and say I was too OCD.

"You're right," JP says. "Last week I was copy editing an article about people who sell their homes and travel around the country in motorhomes. Most of the people featured in the article were retired, but then there was a profile of a professional woman in her thirties. She's a life-coach who does all her work online. She described how she can work in her RV or, better yet, at the beach or in the middle of the   forest, because all she needs is Wi-Fi, and she can get that almost anywhere. As I rearranged her sentences, I felt this rumble of excitement in the base of my stomach."

I listen to JP and watch her as she talks. I can't remember when I last saw her look that animated. Even when Lizzie was alive, I always wondered if maybe JP was a bit depressed because she never seemed excited or happy about anything. I figured she was just a serious kind of person. Certainly, she's intense. But her eyes have lit up and I can see she's genuinely found something that's piqued her interest.

"Have you started looking for an RV?"

"No. I'd rent one first. See if I like it. Then maybe if I do, I'll sell the house and go on the road for a while."

I feel as if she's thumped me in the gut. If she sells the house, every remnant of Lizzie will disappear.

"I can't stay here forever," JP says in a low voice, and I know she's right. She does need to move on. After all, if she stayed here, eventually she'd get involved with someone else and I don't think I'd feel any better about seeing a replacement for Lizzie in this house.

I nod. "I understand. Really I do."

"I've already started cleaning out cupboards and closets. It's a way to feel like I'm moving ahead. I have something that's going to make you very happy."

JP leaves the room, and when she comes back in, she's carrying a small wooden box.

"Your mom's jewelry box." She smiles and thrusts it at me. "And in it, the emeralds you were looking for."

I'm about to tell her that Mom never had a box like that, but I'm so excited about seeing the jewelry that I pull the box toward me and open it. Sure enough Mom's ring and bracelet are there, along with a pin in the shape of a heart, which I've never seen before.

"Would you like this?" I hold out the heart to her, presuming she was the one who gave it to my sister.

"Take a piece of your mom's jewelry? Of course not."

I'm positive it's not a family heirloom, but JP seems unfamiliar with it too, and I don't want to draw any attention to that fact.

I take the box to my bedroom, wondering as I walk down the hallway, who gave Lizzie the diamond heart.

If it wasn't JP was it Jim?

☙

The next morning when I come downstairs, JP has already brewed coffee and there's a platter of bagels, lox and the fixings that go with them.

"What a big breakfast on a day when we're probably going to overeat all day long." I laugh as I pour orange juice into a tall glass.

"I want to finish cleaning out the basement and the garage. That way I reckon we'll have earned our dinner."

It's a relief to be doing something active instead of sitting around trying to make conversation, so I'm happy to lug old cans of paint and primer up the basement steps along with carpet remnants and wallpaper scraps. JP says she's going to put all their camping gear on Craigslist for sale unless I want it. Since my idea of camping is a Holiday Inn Express, I'm happy to let someone who'd enjoy them have the tents, tarps and lantern. I organize the toolbox while JP sorts through jars of screws and nails. When the shelves in the basement are bare, we move on to the garage. We throw out half-used cans of motor oil and antifreeze, and then JP approaches several large plastic tubs. "This is all stuff we never even unpacked after we moved into this house." There are clocks and pictures, candleholders, and even some books. One of them is Lizzie's high school yearbook.

"You want this?" JP hands it to me. "You probably knew some of those people." I flip open the book and facing me is the first boy Lizzie dated. Another page is filled with the girls who used to sit in our kitchen and fight over a plate of Mom's cookies. Lizzie was in her last year of high school when Mom and Dad died, and the messages her friends wrote are filled with condolences and loving thoughts for her future. What would they think if they knew that less than 20 years after they penned those messages, Lizzie is gone?

And how would they react if someone told them she might have been poisoned and the killer is still be on the loose?

Chapter Eleven

"We're running late," Paula says as she welcomes us into their home. "Beth had to run out and get more gas for the barbecue, so we won't be eating for a while. You want to take a walk?"

"Not me," JP says. "I'm gonna head into your back garden and take a nap."

"I'll come," I tell Paula, glad of an opportunity to get to know her better.

It's one of those perfect early-summer days when the sun is warm but the air still has a hint of chill in it. I'm glad I'm wearing a shirt with sleeves instead of the tank top I originally thought I'd wear. I take off at a brisk pace, but Paula walks about half the speed I do, so I slow down.

"How do you think JP's doing?" Paula asks as we walk down a wide street shaded by broad oaks and tall maples.

"It's always a bit hard to know with JP isn't it, but she seems to be doing a lot better. Has she told you her latest plan?"

"About buying an RV? It seems like a good idea."

"I wasn't sure. Part of me wonders if she's running away. I get the feeling she hasn't dealt with her grief, so much as walled it off."

"Being JP, she may never deal with it in the way you mean. Perhaps walling it off is the most she can expect." Paula stops a moment and faces me. "What about you?" Her eyes are full of concern. "How are you doing?"

I shrug. "I have to rejoice in the fact that Lizzie went home to heaven so early."

"You don't sound too happy about it, and I'm not surprised." Paula's voice is surprisingly vehement. "Is that what you've been taught?"

"Of course. I went through all this when my parents died. If you're a Christian, it's selfish to grieve and mourn for oneself when the person who died is in a better place."

"So your feelings don't matter? You don't question why God took such a lovely person from us, way before her time?"

I say nothing. Of course there's a part of me that asks myself that question. But I push it from my mind as unworthy.

"Ashley, can I ask you something?" This is a rhetorical question because before I can answer, she asks anyway. "You seem like such a nice, open person, and I've often wondered how you deal with some of the views of your church."

"I'm not sure what you mean by 'deal with.' If you're a member of the church, you just accept them."

"But if you're a thinking person, surely there are things you must find hard to accept?"

"Yes, of course. But it's not up to me to question. Wasn't that true for you, when you were part of a faith community?"

"Are you kidding? The first rule of Judaism is 'question everything.' Why do you think there are so many Jewish lawyers?" She smiles, and I'm not sure whether she's joking or not. "We were taught that the way to learn is to question. In yeshivas, they put the boys in pairs who spend all morning quizzing each other and each trying to come up with arguments that the other has to refute."

"Isn't that dangerous? I mean, look at you, you're not a believer any more. Too many questions can lead you down the path of doubt."

"Is that a reason to follow things blindly? Shouldn't your beliefs hold up to scrutiny?"

I like Paula, but her views are weird. She almost sounds like an atheist, insisting religion is more like science. I try not to sound impatient when I answer.

"That's the whole point of faith. There are so many things we can't know or prove. You just have to believe there is a   loving God and that Jesus died for our sins."

"But what about the things that aren't about faith— like not accepting gays, or allowing women in positions of leadership?"

I'm starting to sweat and I'm not sure if it's the walk or the talk that's making my skin prickle. "It all has a basis in the Bible. I can show you where those things are proscribed."

"But I can show you things the Bible proscribes that Christians let go of long ago. You don't keep kosher, yet the Bible specifically says you can't eat pork of shellfish. You wear clothes of mixed fibers. You don't stone people. Don't you see how your leaders pick and choose for you?"

Paula is starting to sound like Lizzie. These were the arguments she and I used to have, although they never lasted long because Lizzie would get too frustrated with me and change the subject. At least Paula has a pleasant expression on her face and seems genuinely interested in my views.

"I can't tell you I love everything about Christianity or about our church. I don't like that right now we're having a fundraiser to build a new parking lot, when we could be giving that money to the homeless. I don't like hearing how gay people are depraved. I know enough of you to know that's not true. But you can't pick and choose. If you decide you know better than the Bible, or better than the preachers, who knows where you'd end up?"

Paula laughs. "You sound like the rabbi's wife I used to study with." She sighs. Her expression is one I can't quite figure out, but her eyes look sad.

"Do you miss your religion, Paula?"

She nods. "I do miss some of the rituals. And I miss being part of a larger community. But the good thing about Judaism is that there are many ways to experience it. I'm part of a women's Rosh Hodesh group. We celebrate the New Moon every month. We even have our own prayer book."

"But why, if you don't believe in your religion anymore?"

Paula sighs. "It's complicated. Jews aren't just a religious group, we're also a race. There are Buddhist Jews, Unitarian Jews..."

We've come full circle and are at the end of Paula's street. Someone is waving at us. It's Cleo. She's dressed in a red cotton dress and has a light Mexican shawl draped across her shoulder.

"You two look serious," she says as she approaches.
"Paula was telling me to abandon the church." Paula opens her mouth to respond, but I laugh. "I'm joking." I turn to Cleo. "Does she tell you that too?"
Cleo shakes her head. "She knows singing all those beautiful hymns is the highlight of my week."
"My sentiments exactly." We smile at each other, and immediately I feel a knot in my stomach.

As we walk up the short path to Paula's house, Cleo puts her hand on my shoulder. "It's good to see you again, Ash."

"You too," I mumble then duck indoors quickly.

I'm going to have to put some distance between us. What Cleo may have to offer is nothing I'm willing to accept. Ever.

Chapter Twelve

There's enough food at the picnic to last a month: barbecued meats, veggie skewers, salads, fruit and more pastries than even the school football team could finish. Beth explains that they have the picnic on Saturday so everyone can take leftovers to last the rest of the weekend. When we've eaten our fill, the conversation turns to memories of Lizzie. JP twists a corner of her shirt and bites her lip. I swallow hard, knowing that the reason I'm there is that Lizzie's not. When Paula says it's time to play games, JP asks if I'm okay to leave. I nod and we slip away from the group.

Back at the house, I run upstairs and take out the crinkled piece of paper where I have Jimmy's number. Finally, I have a moment to myself to make the call. My fingers shake as I tap the numbers out on my phone. When a voice answers, I almost hang up, but instead I steel myself and go through with it. As soon as I explain who I am, he begs me to stop by as soon as possible.

"I'm so glad you called," he says. "I can't wait to meet you."

It's not what I expected. Will he be that keen once he knows why I want to talk to him? We arrange to meet at his office in the morning.

§♦

The moment I walk through the door, Jimmy engulfs me in a big bear hug then pushes me back to arm's length.

"The family resemblance is startling. It's almost like having Lizzie in the room."

He has a broad smile and eyes that crinkle in the

corner when he smiles. He's about my age, slightly paunchy and already almost bald.

The large room is flooded with sunshine pouring in through the floor-to-ceiling window. On one side is a massage table with cushions piled in a corner, and on the other, there's a brown suede sofa where Jimmy directs me to sit. In front of it is a thick pile rug. Is this the room where the affair took place?

Jimmy pulls up a stool and sits opposite me.

"I couldn't believe it when Janelle told me about Lizzie," he says, and tears well up in his eyes. "I kept meaning to get in touch with her and now it's too late." He shakes his head from side to side as if he can't believe what he's saying.

"You were really close to her, weren't you?" I say it softly, hoping to encourage him to confide in me.

He nods. "She was like the sister I never had. She was so warm and caring. A lot of my friends in recovery are loud and funny. When they tell their stories, you think you're at a stand-up comedy show. But not Lizzie. She was always   serious about her sobriety."

"And yet she relapsed."

Jimmy's eyes grow wide and his whole body jerks back. "What? I don't believe it."

"You didn't know?"

"I stopped sponsoring her almost two years ago. She was my sponse for almost five years, and she was amazing—so willing to look at her own stuff and take responsibility for her actions. She put some of us to shame. But she outgrew me. I felt I had nothing more to offer her. We'd worked the steps together, twice, and I felt as if she knew more about recovery than I did. Are you sure she relapsed? I mean, I know some of the most surprising people do, but she was so solid in her recovery..." He strokes the top of his bald head from front to back.

"After she was diagnosed with FSGS, Lizzie went out and got drunk. She was intoxicated when they admitted her to the E.R., and JP said she'd slipped several times that year."

Jimmy shakes his head. "You never can tell about people."

He gets up and goes into a little alcove I hadn't noticed

before. He returns a moment later with two cold Cokes. He places then on the table in front of us.

"How come you weren't in touch?" I ask. "Didn't you remain friends after you stopped sponsoring her?"

"We did. But then she made the decision to stop coming to meetings and hanging out with all her AA friends. She said she was ready to move on, and that she wanted to focus on friends who didn't talk about alcohol all the time. It's something we old-timers deal with a lot: whether to stay in the program and help mentor others or to move on. Some people build their whole lives around AA, but Lizzie didn't want to do that. I encouraged her to try cutting back, maybe show up to a meeting once a month or come to the round-up, but she said she wanted to make a clean break."

"Ironic, given what happened after that."

"In some ways, but in others that's exactly why we encourage folks not to abandon the program altogether. Sounds like getting this diagnosis really threw her for a loop."

"Yes." I pop the tab on my Coke and take a large slug. The bubbles fizz up my nose and make me cough. "Though I had no idea she'd taken it so hard. When we spoke on the phone she was very reassuring."

"That was Lizzie though, wasn't it? Always taking care of everyone else."

"Yes. So when she dropped out, you just stopped having any contact?"

"To tell you the truth, I took her decision personally. She did reach out to me once, but I ignored her. She tried again, and then I guess she got the message because I didn't hear from her after that. After I'd simmered down, I kept meaning to call her. It was always going to be next week..."

His voice is filled with regret and he stares into the distance.

I stand up and walk over to the window then turn and ask him, "When you two were working together, was there anything more to it?"

Jimmy looks at me quizzically. "What do you mean?"

"When Lizzie was dying, she told me—or at least I think she told me—that she'd had an affair."

"And you think it was with me?" Jimmy looks incredulous. "Why?"

"I thought she said your name."

A shadow crosses Jimmy's face. I feel awkward, now that I've put him on the spot.

"Lizzie was a lesbian," he says. "You know that."

"She wasn't always a lesbian. JP was the first woman she was ever with. Before that, she was married to a man. Maybe she was bisexual."

"If so, she never told me. She never mentioned an affair either."

"So it wasn't you?"

"Honey, you're barking up completely the wrong tree. I'm a proud asexual man. I like both women and men, but I'm not sexually attracted to either. I don't sleep with people, and I don't have affairs."

A proud asexual man? I have no idea what that means, but he has such an open demeanor that I believe him immediately when he says he wasn't Lizzie's lover.

Jimmy gets up and comes over to where I'm standing.

"Why was it so important for her to tell you about the affair? Was she consumed with guilt for keeping a secret? In AA we tell people 'we're only as sick as our secrets.' Maybe she thought somehow she'd be cured if she told you."

I shrug. How much should I tell him? "I don't think it was that. It sounded like she'd already told JP, or at least that JP knew about it."

"Then how come you haven't asked JP who Lizzie had the affair with?"

"Because then I'd have to tell her what else Lizzie said, and I'm afraid to. You should have seen JP that first day Lizzie died—she went berserk. She was in the yard screaming and throwing dirt. I don't want her to have some kind of nervous breakdown. You can't imagine how upset she was about Lizzie."

"I don't get it. If JP already knows about the affair, why would she be even more upset if she knew Lizzie told you about it on her deathbed?"

Should I tell him? I like him a lot, but I don't think I'm ready to bring up the whole poison thing. Especially since I still don't know who might have done it.

"So if it's not you, is there anyone else in her life by the name of Jim?"

"Is that who she mentioned when she was dying?" He looks at me with a certain expression in his eyes that I can't make out.

"Do you know who she meant?"

"Maybe. When you said Jim, I can tell you what instantly went through my mind."

My heart skips a beat. Am I finally going to get to the bottom of all this?

"Her third love. The first was JP, the second was literature. And then there was her third love. Not Jim, the gym. She swore it was what kept her sane. I'm not sure you could say she was having an affair with the gym, though she probably spent more time at the gym than she ever did with any lover. Do you think she was telling you something about the gym?"

My heart plummets. I was so hopeful when I thought he might know who Lizzie was talking about. Clearly this isn't it.

"I don't think so. She was talking about a person, about...something they might have done."

"Maybe it was someone who goes to the gym?"

Could that be it? It does make sense that she wasn't with another man, but instead of telling me about the gym, why not give me the name of the lover or poisoner?

"Are you sure she didn't say any other name?" Jimmy asks.

I rack my brains and all of a sudden I feel like I've been punched in my gut. She did say something that surprised me. She mentioned Hell. I thought she was having a crisis of faith. What if she didn't mean that at all? I'm fairly sure she said something about 'hell and...' but I couldn't make out what came next. What if that wasn't what she said at all? I think back to the memorial. To the very first person who introduced herself and said she had met my sister at the gym.

What if Lizzie wasn't talking about the afterlife at all, but was simply trying to give me the name of her lover: Helen?

Chapter Thirteen

Jimmy's revelation about Jim being "the gym" has me thinking that I definitely need to go there and take a look at it. I also have to find a way to connect with Helen before I leave, and time is running out. Hopefully, I can kill two birds with one stone. Paula gives me her phone number and I call. I tell Helen that I'm desperate for a good workout.

"I've eaten so much this weekend and will be sitting on a plane all day tomorrow. Does your gym give guest passes?"

She says that they do, and that she'll pick me up in fifteen minutes, which is perfect.

Five minutes later she calls back. "Would you like to go for an outdoor run? It's such a perfect day for it." Is there a reason she doesn't want to take me to the gym? I really want to see it, but it's more important to see Helen so I agree to the run instead. Maybe afterward, I can persuade her to take me by the gym.

I put on my sports bra, a lightweight hoodie, and the multicolored leggings Lizzie mailed me for Christmas last year. By the time I'm ready, Helen's sage green Fiat 500 is at the door.

"Have you ever run the Wissahickon Trail?" she asks as we pull up in a small parking lot that abuts a large wooded area.

"Lizzie and I used to run whenever I visited. We ran in Fairmount Park and down the Drives, but it's been awhile."

Once out of the car I do a few stretches, reaching above my head and down to my toes, twisting my torso to loosen up my back. The air is mild and the lightest of

Alison R. Solomon

breezes plays across my face. It reminds me a little of the Sierra foothills, except that instead of a big blue sky, it's overcast. We start jogging on a gravel path by the side of a pretty creek. It's rained recently and there's a rich fragrance of earthy moisture in the air.

"I remember what you said about Lizzie, at the memorial," I say. "You were the first one to talk, and I could see right away how close you'd been."

"I miss her. For years we stood side by side opposite the mirrors doing our Zumba classes. Zumba Step was our favorite. If one of us was tired, the other would encourage her to keep going. She liked the rhythm of the cumbria and I love the salsa. We both adored the Latino energy and vibe. I always thought we'd be doing those dance classes together until we were old and our knees gave out."

"Instead, my sister died."

"Well yes, but she stopped doing the classes when JP started coming to the gym."

"JP came with her?"

"Yeah. For years Lizzie said working out wasn't JP's scene. Then all of a sudden, she started coming with Lizzie."

My pulse quickens in my chest. Did JP find out Helen and Lizzie were having an affair? Is that why she joined the gym, to keep an eye on them? Or to keep Lizzie away from Helen?

"When JP joined, Lizzie switched up her routine. Started going on the treadmills, which she'd always told me she found boring. Perhaps with JP next to her, she had someone to keep her mind off the monotony. I don't think it was that much of a workout for Lizzie, but I guess she was just so pleased JP was there, that she humored her."

Is that it, or did JP tell Lizzie that if she wanted to keep going to that gym, she had to stay away from Helen?

"They always ended with a swim. JP was a strong swimmer. She would power up and down the lanes doing her freestyle, while Lizzie took her time doing a few laps of backstroke. JP had only been coming for a month or so before Lizzie passed away. I've never seen her there since."

It's hard to talk and run at the same time, and Helen goes silent, probably catching her breath. The trees are loaded with new leaves and make the path

65

dark and almost foreboding.

We slow down a little to run beneath a covered bridge, and I rack my brains to come up with a tactful way to draw Helen out about Lizzie.

"Do you find yourself expecting to see Lizzie when you go to work out? I know whenever my phone rings I still think *maybe it's Lizzie,* and then I have to remind myself that it'll never be Lizzie."

"Yes. That's exactly how I feel. Especially since the whole thing was so incredibly sudden. When Paula called to invite me to the memorial, I was so shocked I literally felt my knees buckle beneath me. I had no idea Lizzie was even in the hospital—none of us did."

Up until now, I hadn't thought about why none of Lizzie's friends had come to the hospital. I'd assumed that only close relatives were allowed to visit. Perhaps the hospital would have allowed Lizzie's friends to visit, but I'm sure JP preferred having no one else around. The last thing she'd have been capable of was making small talk, and I don't think anyone could have helped her feel any better.

"Not being able to say goodbye to Lizzie was awful," Helen says. "When my colleague at work had an aneurysm, our entire department trooped over to the hospital and bid her farewell before they turned off her life support. It was really upsetting to hear about Lizzie after it was all over."

I keep my gaze straight ahead and my pace steady.

"Were you especially close with Lizzie? More than some of the others at the memorial?"

"I like to think so. Although maybe I shouldn't say that. We all had different relationships with Lizzie. I just saw more of her than, say, the people in her book club."

"Did you ever socialize outside of the gym?"

"Yes. After about a year of doing classes together, we got into the habit of having a smoothie at the cafe in the fitness center. Then one day, Lizzie asked me if I wanted to mix it up and go for a coffee."

"Was she..." It's hard for me to say the words, but I do it anyway. "Was she coming on to you?"

Helen snorts. "Lizzie? Are you kidding me? Lizzie would never be unfaithful to JP." She narrows her eyes which have an expression of annoyance. "Actually, I can't believe you would ask me that. You're her sister. You knew her. Why would you even say something like that?"

I don't want to besmirch Lizzie's name by telling too many people about her infidelity, but I do need to know why Helen is so defensive.

"I didn't mean to upset you. I heard that something had happened. And it sounded like it might be with someone from her gym."

Helen stops in place and spins around to face me. "You don't know me, Ashley, or you would know that I would never, ever be with someone who was in a relationship. But you do know your sister, and if someone is spreading rumors about her, you should be asking yourself why. Your sister is dead and you're listening to gossip? How dare you call yourself a Christian."

She takes off, sprinting away from me. I'm shocked at the intensity of her reaction. Is she hiding something? Have I touched on a nerve?

I sprint ahead to catch up to her. I'm going to have to come clean.

"It's not gossip, Helen. Lizzie herself told me."

Helen pulls to a halt, bends over, and puts her hands on her knees. "She told you? When?"

"In the hospital." I have to tread carefully. I don't want to tell her anything about my suspicions.

But all she says is, "So it's true."

Which doesn't make her sound like the mystery lover.

"You knew?" I mirror her posture, put my hands on my knees, then straighten up.

"There were rumors, about a year ago. Someone at the gym said they were at a gay bar up in New Hope and thought they saw her slow dancing with a woman who wasn't JP. They saw her leave with that same woman. I rushed to her defense and said she was probably just getting a ride home."

A year ago. That's when Lizzie was diagnosed, the same time JP said she'd had a relapse.

I walk over to the nearby bench and sit down. Helen joins me.

"It wasn't like Lizzie doing something like that," she says. "She adored JP." She pauses, looks at the azaleas growing wild at our side. "I'm going to tell you something

I've never told anyone else."

"Whatever it is, it's just between us," I assure her.

She takes a deep breath. "Early on when I met Lizzie, I did flirt with her. She was everything I thought I might want in a woman. She nipped it in the bud right away. She was nice about it, but she made it clear she would never, ever betray JP. That's why I got so defensive before."

"You said she was coming out of a bar. JP told me she relapsed a year before she died. Maybe that was when it happened. Maybe she was drunk."

"A drunken one-night stand would sure make more sense than an ongoing affair." She looks as if she wants to say more.

I wait but she stands and starts warming up again. "You ready to run some more?"

I join her and we resume jogging. The sun has burst through the clouds, and now the leafy trees offer welcome shade.

"When I heard Lizzie had died, I couldn't believe it. It seemed crazy that she was admitted to the hospital the same day she'd been at the gym."

"You know for sure she was at the gym?" I ask, as I undo the zipper on my hoodie.

"Yes. I saw her. That's why I was so devastated when I heard."

I'm starting to get more and more confused. It's hard enough to believe Lizzie got drunk the day she was admitted to the hospital. Knowing that she'd been at the gym earlier that day makes it even weirder.

Could something have happened at the gym that would have upset Lizzie? Was the woman she slept with in New Hope there? "You said someone at the gym saw her at that bar in New Hope. Did he know the woman she left with?"

Helen screws up her face in thought. "I can ask him." She says. "But what difference would it make?"

I can't think of anything to say.

Helen stops and faces me. "I understand," she says. "You want to know everything you can about your sister's life."

I nod in agreement. But it's not her life I want to know about. It's her death.

Chapter Fourteen

JP makes us sandwiches with Beth's leftover barbecue and serves them on paper plates. If Lizzie were here, she'd have used china and had freshly baked cookies on hand for dessert. The kitchen would have felt warm and inviting. Instead it feels functional, with a vague aroma of bleach.

JP takes a bite of sandwich and asks, "How was your run with Helen?"

I'd been wondering how I was going to bring this up. "Great. She told me how much she misses Lizzie."

"I bet she does. I always thought she had a bit of a crush on her."

"Really? Did you mind?"

"Nah. I knew it wasn't reciprocated." She takes a big bite of sandwich and wipes brown sauce off her chin.

"Helen told me you'd joined the gym they used to go to. She said she hasn't seen you there since...since Lizzie passed."

JP grimaces. "I only went to keep Lizzie company."

"Or perhaps to keep an eye on her," I say in a joking tone. "If you thought all the ladies were after her."

JP's eyes narrow. "That's bullshit."

Did I hit a sore spot? I change the subject quickly. "Helen said Lizzie was at the gym the very day she died."

"Yeah. She went almost every day, so that's hardly surprising."

"Did anything happen there?"

"What do you mean?"

"It seems odd that she was feeling good enough to go to the gym but later she got drunk. Do you think something happened that upset her?"

JP looks a little startled and shakes her head. "I don't think so."

"But if she was at the gym earlier that day, what would have caused her to go out and start drinking? It doesn't make any sense."

JP frowns. "What's going on? Why are you suddenly honing in on all of this?"

I take a deep breath. It's time to come clean. "There's something I haven't told you. About when Lizzie died. I didn't want to upset you, so I didn't see any point in saying anything. Now I have to."

JP looks at me. "Go on," she says, her expression still wary.

"Before she died, Lizzie tried to tell me something. It was really hard to make out. But...I think she was trying to tell me that someone had poisoned her."

"*What?*" JP's face grows red and I can't tell if she's shocked or angry.

"I can't be sure. It's just...that's what it sounded like."

"And did she tell you who it was who tried to take this melodramatic action?" JP's tone is dripping sarcasm.

"She didn't tell me exactly. But she said something about having an affair, and it sounded like maybe whoever she'd had the affair with—"

JP laughs. "You know they had her doped up on drugs, don't you?"

"But...you knew there was an affair?"

"Oh, I knew alright."

"Do you know who it was with? Is it possible that person tried to poison her?"

It's such a relief to have told JP. I didn't realize what a heavy weight the burden of secrecy had placed on me. Finally I can get some help from the person who may be as invested as I am in finding out the truth.

"I don't want to talk about her infidelity."

"No, of course not, and I don't want to pry. I just thought—"

"The only person who poisoned Lizzie, was Lizzie. By drinking."

"So you don't think that person, whoever it was..."

"I don't know who it was, okay? I didn't want to know. But it was over. She told me. I forgave her, and we put it behind us."

"But what do you think she was trying to tell me?"

JP says nothing, and suddenly a thought comes slamming into my brain. "Had she already mentioned poison to you?"

JP looks scornful. "No. And if she had, I'd have asked them to decrease the drugs she was on."

"I wonder why she told me and not you," I muse. All of a sudden a realization sweeps over me and I feel like I can hardly breathe.

"Oh my God, JP, I'm so sorry. Of course it wasn't *me* she was trying to tell. It was you. She must have realized how close she was to dying, so she wanted to tell you. She kept saying your name. But you weren't there, so she had to tell me instead." I feel tears forming in my eyes and brush them away, furious with myself. "Please, forgive me. I should have told you from the start."

JP is looking at me with the strangest expression. Her face has gone pale and she looks as if she wants to throw up. I wait for her to speak but she says nothing. I can't believe what an idiot I've been. No wonder she's upset. All this time I was meant to pass on the message, and I never did.

"Forgive me, JP, I was trying to spare your feelings. But now that you know all about it, we can work together, right? I can tell you everything I've already tried to figure out and—"

"Shut up, Ashley. Just *shut up*." JP's voice is low, and for a moment it almost feels threatening. "Nobody poisoned Lizzie and there's nothing to find out. She must have been delirious."

"But—"

"If Lizzie really thought she'd been poisoned, she could have told me when we first got to the E.R. or she could have told the doctor or one of the nurses." JP's tone is a little more forgiving and the expression on her face is one of sympathy. "I know you lost your sister, but you need to deal with it, not start dredging up a bunch of nonsense. You can talk to me about Lizzie if it helps, but I don't want to hear anything more about poison and murder. Nobody killed my wife. I won't entertain that thought for one moment, and neither should you."

JP picks up her plate, sweeps her half-eaten sandwich into the garbage and begins to clear off the rest of the table.

"Maybe you should join a grief group or see a therapist. You've blown everything way out of proportion."

᠔᠊

As I pack up my small suitcase, ready to make an early start the next morning for the airport, I can't help wondering if JP's right. I thought she'd be as invested as I am in finding out the truth, but she made me feel like I'm crazy. Am I? Dr. Lim implied the same thing: that grief was making me illogical and maybe even nuts.

I look around the room to ensure I've packed everything. I almost forgot the carved jewelry box sitting on the nightstand. I pick it up carefully and place it in my suitcase. I still wonder why JP assumed the box was Mom's. Did Lizzie tell her that, and if so, why? I open the box and stare at Mom's ring and bracelet and again at that diamond heart. The heart obviously meant something to Lizzie, but what? I close the box and get ready for bed. It's been a very long weekend, and I'm ready to head home.

Chapter Fifteen

By the time I arrive at my apartment, I'm bone tired. I have to wade through a pile of newspapers because I forgot to cancel them, and I've already picked up an armful of mail from the mailbox downstairs. I drag my suitcase into the bedroom, where I would like to jump straight into bed. It's early evening in California, and I need to get back on Pacific Time or I'll end up awake at 3:00 a.m. I open the suitcase and start to pull my clothes out of it. The capris and blouse I wore to the picnic make me think of the conversation I had with Paula before the picnic. I wouldn't admit it to her, but I do sometimes struggle with loving a God who has caused me so much pain. Losing my parents was terrible enough, but to lose my sister as well? My faith tells me He loved her so much, He didn't want to wait for her to get old, yet that makes Him sound selfish. Surely there are enough amazing souls in heaven that my sister could have walked this earth a little longer. People say tragedies help us grow strong, but sometimes I wish I weren't being so harshly tested.

I put away the rest of my clothes and turn the suitcase upside down to make sure there's nothing left in it. Something clatters to the floor, and too late, I remember the jewelry box. The contents spill out. I kneel down to gather up Mom's ring and bracelet and the diamond heart. The velvet lining they were resting on has also come out. I pick up the box and as I start to replace the lining, I spot something in the box underneath the velvet. I sit back on my haunches and take a closer look.

It's a small notecard with a drawing of a blossoming iris on it. I flip it over expecting to see the name of the artist on the back. Instead there's a handwritten message.

"Nothing is ever bad enough to end your life over. I'm crazy about you, but whether or not we ever get together again, you need to leave JP. Whatever you decide, I'll be here. Whatever you need."

I read it twice, too stunned to believe what I'm seeing. She talked about killing herself.

Over and over I keep repeating in my head: *she had an affair and then considered suicide.*

The well of sadness inside me descends so deep, it feels bottomless. Lizzie was in such pain and yet she didn't confide in me. She thought I would say what our church teaches: that we have no more right to take our own lives than we do to take someone else's. That suicide is still murder, even if it's self-murder, and that she would be doomed for eternity. I don't know if that's what I'd have said. I never had the chance to find out.

So many questions are spinning through my mind that I can barely catch on to them. Why was Lizzie thinking about ending her life? She had a job she loved, good friends and a loyal wife. Yet the writer of the note believed she should leave JP. Lizzie never mentioned having any problems at home. She'd even told me that once she was diagnosed with FSGS, JP had been more loving and attentive than ever.

If only I knew who wrote the note. I have to find out. Somehow I have to track down this woman. It's too late to call Helen now, but I'll call tomorrow and see if she was able to get any information from her source at the gym.

Meanwhile, the box and its contents lead me to more questions. Why did Lizzie keep the note? If she was so sure she would always stay with JP, why not throw it out, or burn it? Was she considering leaving JP? Did she want it as a reminder of how low she'd felt?

And why did Lizzie let JP think the jewelry box itself was Mom's? The obvious answer is that she didn't want JP to look inside, but it wasn't locked. JP had opened it and seen the diamond heart, which she assumed was a family heirloom. I know it's crazy, but I can't help wondering if all of this was some kind of message for me.

The moment I have that thought, an image comes to mind from years ago: me and Lizzie sorting through Mom's stuff after she died. We were in such pain after our parents' funeral that it took us days to start going through their things. When we found Mom's jewelry box, there were two envelopes inside, one for Dad and one inscribed with our names. Dad never got to see his. We both agreed it was private, and we never read it. Inside our envelope there was a love note to both of us. "You are the diamonds in my heart," she wrote. That's why the brooch was in the box. She wanted me to remember Mom's note and look for a note from her. If I hadn't dropped the box, eventually I'd have figured it out and taken the box apart to look for a note. If anything ever happened to her, Lizzie wanted me to find the notecard. Which leaves one massive, glaring question dancing in front of my eyes.

Why would Lizzie think something might happen?

The next day at school, I'm preoccupied with thoughts about the note. I force myself to deal with all the odds and ends I need to tie up before the end of the year, but my mind keeps wandering, and I can't wait to get home. School's closing early today for an in-service I don't need to attend, but at the last minute I remember I have to run choir practice. When we're done, I pack up the music stands as fast as I can.

Jordan, the kid with the father who doesn't like vegetarians, helps me put everything away. When we're finished, he sidles up to me and asks, "Can I talk to you, Miss Glynn, in your office?"

It's the last thing I want to do right now, but I never say no when a kid reaches out. I invite him to sit down and bring him a bottle of water. He's tall and gangly, with the usual teenage smattering of acne on his forehead. He scratches at one of the pimples, and I want to tell him to stop, it'll make it worse, although that's the last thing he wants to hear right now.

"What's up, buddy?" I sit down opposite him. "How was Memorial Day?"

"Good and bad," he says.

I look at him questioningly and hope my expression will invite him to continue.

"It's always the same, like a ping-pong game with me and my brother watching the show. Dad tries to make me eat hot dogs, and Mom grills veggie burgers. Dad says how proud he is of Bob for getting perfect grades in his first semester at   college, and Mom jumps in to remind Dad that I made Varsity."

"So was that the good or the bad?" I smile.

He shares the joke for a moment, then looks serious. "If I tell you something, you don't have to share it with anyone else do you?"

Uh-oh. "Depends what you tell me. If you're thinking about hurting yourself or someone else, then yes, I do."

His eyes grow wide. "No, nothing like that."

"We have a professional counselor on staff. Have you talked to her?"

He shakes his head. "I sounded her out, without telling her anything. She just spouts the party line."

"And you think I won't?"

Part of me wonders whether I should be encouraging him to talk to me, because whatever this is, it sounds like it might be complicated. But I'm starting to get curious.

"The good part of my holiday was that I met someone. Someone I really like. A lot."

Relief floods through me. I can deal with the angst of teenage romance pretty easily.

"That's great, Jordan. Tell me about her."

Jordan looks up at me. "Not her. Him. I really like this boy I met."

I can see fear and hope in his eyes. He's dreading that I'll be like all the other people in his life who would come down on him like a ton of bricks. But he's hoping that his choice of confidante was right.

"Does he like you too?"

"Yes. We hung out together all day Sunday, and it was like we were instantly best friends."

"Oh." Again I'm flooded with relief. "So you're just good friends then."

He looks taken aback. "No. That's what made it so cool—we made out and stuff, and we really like each other."

Shit. "It sounds like it's not the first time you've made out with a boy then?" I can't believe I'm even asking this question. I've got used to being around Lizzie and her friends, but I've never in my life talked to a gay male. Not that Jordan is necessarily gay. He's only fifteen after all. Plenty of time to change.

"Right. Up until now it's just been a grope in the locker room, touching in the dark... that kind of thing. Then one of us always says, 'I won't say anything if you don't' or 'this doesn't mean we're faggots.' All the usual stuff. But Austin and me, we already know we're in love."

"Wow," I say, at a loss for anything else.

"I know. I feel like I'm jumping high as the moon, except I'm scared shitless at the same time. My dad would literally kill me if he knew. Even my mom would kick me out of the house."

"Our parents don't always react the way we think they will," I say. My mouth tastes bitter. My own parents never had a chance to demonstrate whether that was true.

"Austin's parents are cool with him. They go to a totally different kind of church than we do. He told me all about it. They call themselves 'welcoming' and it means they welcome gay people. Can you imagine? I couldn't believe it when he told me. I can't imagine our church being like that in a million years."

He's right about that. We believe in the sanctity of heterosexual marriage and anything else will never fly.

"How did you meet Austin?"

"That's what's so completely amazing. His family moved into a house on our street. He only lives three doors away. It would be easy to let Mom and Dad think we're just best buds, but I don't like lying to them, especially Mom. She already figured out something's up. She asked me if I met a girl. I kinda let her think I had, because I didn't want to have to tone myself down."

"I don't think you should say anything to them."

"You don't approve." He looks crestfallen. "You think I'm perverted. You think the same as everyone else."

"I didn't say that. I know gay people and I don't think they're depraved. But I know our community, and I know our church, and to me it makes no sense for you to tell anyone. You're young, you have the whole world before you. Kids your age fall in and out of love all the time. I know you think Austin's 'The One,' but he might not be. This time next year it could be someone completely different."

"It won't be." He looks crestfallen. "Austin said there had to be someone at school I could trust, and I thought of you. You're different from everyone else. I know you're not married and..." He shakes his head back and forth. "Whatever," he mutters.

"What on earth does my not being married have to do with anything?" I shouldn't be defending myself right now, but what does he mean? Jordan says nothing, just scratches awkwardly at one of his pimples. There's a silence and then it dawns on me. "You thought I was gay?"

"Forget it." He gathers up sheet music. "Just forget I ever told you anything." He stands up, pushes his chair back, and walks out of my office.

I tilt back in my chair. Do they all think that? I know how kids talk. And what about the other teachers. Do they think that too? Do they talk about me behind my back, secretly wondering about the spinster music teacher? I hear myself say the words and think, shit, how much more of a stereotype can you get?

Chapter Sixteen

I call Helen as I'm driving home. Amazingly she has news for me. The guy at the gym, who saw Lizzie at the bar, talked to someone who talked to someone, and Helen has a name and an email address for me.

"I can't believe it," I tell her. "It's only been a couple of days."

She assures me that the gay world is a small one, especially since the gay bar was in a small town.

I spend an hour crafting an email to TaniaT123. I need to get the tone right. I can't let this mystery woman know that I have any suspicions, but I need to pique her interest enough that she'll respond. In the end, I tell her simply that I have the notecard she sent Lizzie, that I'd like to discuss its contents with her, and that anyone who cared so much about my sister is a friend of mine.

I spend the rest of the afternoon unable to settle into anything. I go for a run, but after a couple of circuits around my local park, I'm exhausted.

I have to keep busy so I pull together the ingredients to bake lemon bars, even though I have no idea who I'll share them with. Nothing about them goes right. The pastry dough is so dry it crumbles when I press it into the pan, so I add water which makes a sticky mess. The topping is way too runny, but I can't remember how to correct it. I shove the pan into the oven and then burst into tears.

I miss Lizzie so much I don't think I can bear it. When I used to wake up in the night and Daddy would come to comfort me I'd whine, "I want my mommy." That's how I feel now, except it's Lizzie I want. I feel so alone in the world.

I go to my bookcase and start straightening each tome until I have a rigid line. I'm just done, when I smell burning. I throw out the scorched lemon bars then sit at my kitchen table, drumming my fingers impatiently on the laptop. I'm rewarded when all of a sudden a notification appears on the desktop. TaniaT123 has sent me a message!

I'm so glad you reached out to me. I couldn't believe it when I heard about Lizzie.

It's so unexpected my fingers shake as I reply.

Can we message instead of email?

She agrees and for the next half hour messages fly back and forth.

Was it just one night?

Yes. I flirted with her at the club. Then we went back to my place. We had a good time, but she wasn't really into it. I asked her if she needed to talk and she said yes.

What did she tell you?

She was upset because she'd just received a serious   medical diagnosis. She was worried that she would end up being a burden on her wife. I asked how come she was at my house if she had a wife, and she got really upset and said she'd screwed everything up. Then she started talking about how she should just end it all. I don't know if it was just the booze making her say that.

Did you stay in touch?

She called me the next day from work. Said JP got ugly with her when she got home and I shouldn't contact her again. I told her to leave; nobody should ever put up with that kind of crap. She said JP was just upset, she'd never done anything like that before. Said she loved JP and asked me to respect her wishes.

But you sent the card?

I was worried about her. I sent it to her work.

Did she respond?

She called a few days later. JP had given her the silent treatment for days and then forgiven her completely. I said that sounded like an abuser to me, and she said no, I had it all wrong. JP was treating her like a queen. Said it was all her fault because she'd been drinking, and that she would never drink again. I begged her to call me if anything ever happened. She promised me she would.

And did she?

I never heard from her again. When I saw her obituary in The Lavender News, I was shocked.

I'm shaking so badly after this conversation I don't know what to do. Lizzie said she'd never drink again and yet she did. At least once when she ended up in the E.R., and maybe other times too. Was she really one of those alcoholics who, however much they try, can't stay sober? The most troubling part of the call is the fact that JP "got ugly" with Lizzie. What did that mean? Whatever happened, it leads to another question. How could JP have been so upset with Lizzie and then managed to forgive her so quickly and completely?

I consider calling Paula, but then I remember that TaniaT123 mentioned calling Lizzie at work. Perhaps Cleo overheard something. I decide it's not too late in the evening to call, so I pick up the phone. I'm relieved when Cleo answers on the first ring.

"Did I wake you?" I ask. My heart is thudding and I don't know if it's because of what I'm going to ask, or simply because I'm talking to Cleo.

"No, I was just cleaning the kitty litter. Is it something urgent?"

"Did Lizzie ever confide in you about any problems she might have had in her relationship?"

There's a silence on the line.

"I know there was an issue," I say, "about a year ago, around the time Lizzie was diagnosed. I need to find out more about it."

"This sounds like a face-to-face conversation. Can I Skype you in five minutes?"

I stare at the computer screen until I hear the familiar Skype tone ringing. I jab my finger on the video icon and come face-to-face with Cleo, who looks even more perfect than usual. Her black braids are wrapped with little, colorful beads that accentuate her dark eyes. My heart starts hammering and I take some deep breaths.

"You look as if you've been crying," she says. "It's still a shock to me when I see you in person. You and Lizzie were so alike, it's almost as if I'm talking to her."

"Even when I look like this, with red eyes and a blotchy face?"

"I saw Lizzie like that once or twice too. Talking of Lizzie, what did you want to know?"

"Did she and JP ever go for couples counseling?"

Cleo shakes her head. "They were happy together. Lizzie was one of the most content people I knew. I mean apart from when..." Her voice trails off.

"When she got sick? She was always upbeat with me. But did you see a different side?"

"At first she worried that she was going to be a burden on JP. I had to keep reminding her that JP was her spouse and that marriage is for better and for worse."

"Do you think anything changed between them after she got the diagnosis?"

"I think it made them bond even more." A cat mews in the background. Cleo turns around to look for it and clicks her fingers, calling it to her.

"You make them sound like the perfect couple."

"They were—although they had their moments. I remember one day when Lizzie came to work all upset. She and JP had argued. But within a few days they were right as rain and even closer than ever." She twirls her braids around her middle finger.

"She certainly seemed genuinely devastated by Lizzie's

illness and passing."

Cleo looks puzzled. "Why wouldn't she be?" The cat mews again and Cleo bends down to pick it up. She puts the large ginger tabby on her lap and starts stroking it absently. "Did you ever overhear any phone calls that made you think there could be trouble in paradise? Another woman..."

"You think one of them had an affair?" Cleo pushes her braids back behind her ears and leans in toward the screen. "I don't know who's been telling you that, but I don't think you should listen." She says. "Lizzie and JP were devoted to each other."

What would she think if I told her about TaniaT123 and the note card? I need to have someone's help with all this, but if Lizzie didn't share her secrets with Cleo, it doesn't seem right that I would. Part of me wants to have every excuse in the world to spend more time talking to Cleo and getting to know her.

The other part tells me that's exactly why she's the last person I should be asking for help.

Chapter Seventeen

Work is the one place I can almost stop thinking about Lizzie, so I throw myself into it. While the teachers and the kids are winding down for the end of the year, I work like a crazy person. We're making new, glossy, brochures that need to be available for our end-of-year Open House, and I'm also in the process of nailing down a popular gospel band to provide a concert for us in the Fall. When the school secretary invites me to lunch I tell her I'm too busy.

I'm microwaving a portion of spinach lasagna in the break room, when I hear Luke, who is reading the newspaper, give a little gasp.

"Look at this," he says. I glance over his shoulder.

Mom gets 20 years for poisoning six-year-old son, blares the headline. Please don't say she's one of our parents; I can't make changes to the brochure now. It turns out she's in the mid-West. Luke just wants me to read it because it's so shocking. The article describes a kid who was in and out of the hospital his whole life, but he wasn't really sickly at all. The illnesses he had were all caused by the mom. When her son was still a baby, she persuaded doctors to insert a feeding tube for him, and it just took off from there. She kept making the child sick in a way that the doctors believed was real when in fact she was creating the illnesses. No one realized what was going on until it was too late. They only discovered after he died that his death was caused by the mom putting a deadly amount of salt in his feeding tube.

"What kind of a mother does that?" I shake my head in disbelief. Why have a child, if that's what you end up doing to him?

"It says these kinds of people crave the attention they

get from being the caregiver of a sick child. Everybody gives them sympathy, and they drink it in, like an alcoholic. It's a syndrome called Munchausen by proxy, a mental illness."

"Sounds more like abuse than illness."

"It's both I guess. We should pray for her." Luke folds the paper up, and when the microwave pings, I grab my dish and head back to my office. By the end of the afternoon, Good News gospel choir has confirmed a date for our harvest festival, and I'm thrilled.

℘

Ever since messaging with Tania, I can't stop thinking about how JP treated Lizzie after New Hope. Maybe it was only that one time, but if someone's abusive, they can't usually stop themselves. At home, as I'm getting ready for choir rehearsal, I flash back to the article Luke showed me this morning. A woman who got away with murder. A woman who fooled the doctors. A woman I thought was abusive.

I've been so focused on Lizzie's last days, but what if all of this started way before that? Is there any way someone could have induced Lizzie's FSGS symptoms like that mother did to her son? The moment I have that thought, I feel myself go hot and cold all over. Because the "someone" I'm thinking about would have to be JP. I thought Lizzie's doctors had been remiss in not noticing her FSGS symptoms sooner. *What if that was because she didn't really have FSGS?* What if, somehow, JP did something to create a medical condition that looked like FSGS? The doctors presumed Lizzie's kidney failure was a natural extension of her condition. But could it all have been created by a person who wasn't getting enough attention any other way?

Before I can stop myself, I'm on the Internet, exploring the signs and symptoms of FSGS and kidney disease. I jump when my phone rings and I look down to see Mike's number on the screen.

"Where the heck are you? We're rehearsing the oratorio tonight."

I think quickly. "Sorry. Emergency. Be there in ten

minutes." I hang up, jump in the car, and race to the chapel.

୫♥

The beautiful sound of the oratorio wafts out into the parking lot. Our choir is so amazing when we all blend in harmony together. I listen closely and catch the opening bars of my solo. Damn. Mike's got the second soprano singing it. Her voice is solid, though I like to think I'm better. I slip into the room and am about to take my place when Mike signals me to stay to the side for now. He makes me wait for the rehearsal break before I can join the ranks. Afterward, he asks me to stay behind. I guess I'm in trouble.

"Let's go for coffee," he says.

I don't want to. I want to get straight back to my computer, but it sounds like an order, not an invitation.

It takes forever to leave because Mike has to close up the chapel after everyone has put away the music stands and benches. It's already late by the time he locks the doors.

"Why don't you come back to my place?" he asks.

I try not to look startled even though it's common knowledge that none of us has ever been invited to his home. He's an extremely private person.

I follow Mike back to his condo. When he opens the door, a large, black dog pushes past him and bounds up to me, nuzzling his face on my thigh, as if we are old friends reuniting. I'm gripped by an acute sadness: I have no one in my life who is ever excited to see me and certainly no one who bounds up to me when I come home.

"Don't mind him." Mike grabs his collar and pulls him back so I can come inside.

I'm surprised by the interior of the condo. Mike's always so stern and stiff at rehearsals that I'd pictured something sparse and austere. Instead I'm surrounded by shelves overflowing with knickknacks, tables and chests covered in embroidered cloths, and walls you can barely see for all the pictures.

"I'm glad you're finally here," he says. "I've wanted us to get together for a while."

He has? Then I remember how he invited me to the high school musical. *Oh no! Please don't tell me he's been wanting to date.* Mike is definitely not my kind of guy with his six-foot, bulky frame and his bushy beard. I'm not sure if I have a type, but the last couple of guys I've dated were skinny and clean-shaven.

He asks if I prefer red or white wine and motions me to sit on the blue velvet sofa in the living room. There's a small coffee table in front of me, set on a cream-colored rug. I hear the tinkle of glasses in the kitchen, and Mike appears a couple of minutes later bearing a silver tray laden with wine, cheese and crackers. He puts them in front of us and comes to sit next to me on the sofa. I was hoping he'd sit in the recliner opposite.

"You've changed recently," he says. "You never would have been late for a rehearsal before."

"I know. Stuff on my mind."

"I thought you said it was an emergency."

"Kinda."

"I hope everything's okay now," he says, and pats my knee before handing me the wine glass. "Cheers!" He clinks my glass and as he does, he inches closer to me, so that his thigh rubs against mine.

I feel uncomfortable. I shift away from him a little, almost jamming myself into the arm of the sofa.

"You have a lovely home." I wave my free arm around to incorporate the living room and dining area.

"Would you like to see the rest of it?" He takes the glass from my hand and sets it down on the table. I pick it right back up again. The last thing I want is to be steered toward the bedroom, which is presumably the only other room to see.

"No, I'm good, thanks." I take a gulp of wine and lean forward to place a chunk of Brie on a cracker.

I sense his gaze shift toward the gap in my blouse created by my leaning forward.

"You're really pretty, Ash. I've thought that for a long time."

Please tell me this isn't happening.

A sudden image of Cleo comes to mind, her soft, dark features, her ample breasts beneath that red clingy dress she wore to the picnic. I don't want to encourage Mike, but

I don't want to encourage my own thoughts either. They will lead me down a path I don't want to go.

"Thanks, Mike, I really admire your work as choirmaster. Even though you're tough on us, you're always fair."

"I hope you admire me for other things too," Mike says, edging closer again.

If only it were Cleo. The thought pops into my head, unbidden and unwanted. *Dammit. I'm Christian and I'm straight.*

Mike takes the wineglass out of my hand and turns to kiss me. Instead of pulling away as my instincts tell me, I lean forward and open my lips allowing him in. His mustache scratches my mouth and his tongue feels sharp and tough. I force myself to respond, allowing my tongue to move with his. He pulls me toward him so that he can embrace me. I let him hug me briefly, then I pull away and grab my wineglass.

"Well." I laugh, a false high-pitched giggle. "That was unexpected." I drain my wineglass then lunge forward to grab more cheese, hoping that as long as I eat or drink, it will keep him at bay. He waits for me to swallow my cracker then moves toward me.

"I've wanted to do this for a long time." He moans and pushes his hand beneath my blouse. He grabs my breast and fondles it.

"No!" I push his hand off me. "Don't."

Mike looks taken aback. "Am I going too fast? I can slow down. We don't have to go all the way. Not tonight anyway."

I shake my head. "I'm sorry, Mike, I'm just not attracted to you in that way."

His eyes narrow. "Who *are* you attracted to, Ashley?"

"What do you mean?"

"I mean, I've long suspected you're a dyke. Rumor has it your sister was too. Does it run in the family?"

I slam my glass on the table and it shatters on impact. Shards of glass splinter on the table and onto the rug.

"How dare you? My sister was a lesbian. But that doesn't mean I am."

"Really?" Mike sneers.

"Just because I'm not attracted to you, doesn't mean

I'm not attracted to men."

"Then prove it." Mike lunges at me again and pins me beneath him. One of his hands grabs at my breast while the other tries to lift my chin toward him so that he can kiss me. He's large and heavy, but though I'm small, I learned years ago how to defend myself. In a sudden movement I twist my torso, pull my leg up, and jam my knee into his groin. He yelps and pulls himself up, his hands going instinctively to his privates. I wriggle out from beneath him and tumble onto the floor in the process. I put my hand out to break the fall and feel a piercing pain as it lands on a shard of glass.

"Dammit!" Mike snarls, looking angrily at the bright, red drops of blood spattering his cream carpet. He stumbles out of the living room while I extricate myself from the shards and pull myself up. He reappears with paper towels and a spray bottle and begins picking up the glass and spraying the stain. He ignores me completely.

I don't know what to do. I want to leave, but not like this. Mike's the choirmaster and I'm first soprano. I want things to be okay between us. I wait until he's done cleaning then go up to him and say, "Mike, I'm sorry. I didn't mean to hurt your feelings. I'm sure there's a way for us to deal with this."

He turns, a vicious expression in his eyes, and snorts. "You're right. There *is* a way to deal with this. You're fired from the choir. And if you say one word about why, I'll see you're fired from your job as well." He turns his back to me and mutters, "Fucking ball-breaker."

Chapter Eighteen

I spend a sleepless night, tossing and fretting, wondering what I should do.

I don't want to leave the choir; rehearsals are the highlight of my week, second only to the actual Sunday service. I could ignore Mike's dictate and show up anyway, but he might throw me out in front of everyone, which would be mortifying. I could try to expose him, but what would I say? We weren't on church property, and I agreed to go to his home late in the evening. I should have realized why he invited me back there. I try to tell myself he didn't do anything wrong. If only he'd stopped when I said no, then he wouldn't have been out of order. But he crossed the line and why should he get away with that? He was in the wrong, not me. Why should I be forced to abandon the thing I love, because of something he did?

There has to be a way to sort this out; I need to find someone who could act as a mediator so I can continue in the choir. The obvious person is Pastor Timothy, and the next day finds me walking from my office across the campus to the church admin offices.

"Always a pleasure to see you, my dear." Even though Pastor Timothy must be approaching eighty, his blue eyes still twinkle and his mind is sharp. He baptized me and buried our parents. He's like a kindly grandfather. We exchange pleasantries and then I tell him why I'm there.

"Mike and I had a bit of an awkward incident," I say. "As a result, he doesn't want me in the choir anymore."

Pastor Tim looks astounded. "That's not like Mike. What did you do?"

I bristle under the assumption that I'm in the wrong. "He made advances and I didn't accept them."

"Had you encouraged him to think you were interested?"

Had I? It was a question I asked myself all night when I couldn't sleep. At what point did I give him the wrong impression?

"I don't believe I did. We were at his condo last night and—"

"You went to his condo? At night?"

"It was after choir. I thought he wanted to talk about the fact that I was late for rehearsal."

"You thought he invited you to his home late at night to talk business?" Pastor Timothy smiles at me and I can see he thinks I'm either incredibly naïve, or there's something I'm not telling him. "I can see why he may have got the wrong impression."

I suddenly see myself through Pastor Tim's eyes. A young woman who goes to the apartment of a well-respected man, late in the evening.

"I've known you since you were a little girl. I've always thought you and Mike would make a good couple, and I'm probably not the only one who thought that." I don't understand why he's saying this until he says softly, "Did you change your mind?" I feel like a sleazy call girl who backed out of a contract. Tears spring into my eyes, and I shake my head.

"It's complicated, isn't it, my dear? But it does sound to me like the best thing is indeed for you to discontinue your participation in the choir. At least for now. When all the hurt feelings have dissipated, you can both reexamine the issue. Meanwhile, I'll look forward to seeing you in the pews next Sunday, along with all my other beloved parishioners."

He stands and indicates that our meeting is at an end.

I walk out in a daze. Grace Covenant has been my home for so long. But Pastor Tim and Mike are making me feel like the unwanted stepchild.

§♥

I spend the rest of the week in a fog. When Paula calls to see how I'm doing, I let it go to voicemail. I keep going over the incident with Mike and thinking about my own reactions. I *did* let him kiss me even though I wasn't attracted to him. I did it to try to prove something to myself, which was stupid. I told him that not being attracted to him didn't mean I was attracted to women. But was that true? I keep remembering how Cleo sprang into my mind when I was with Mike. Then, when I think of Cleo, all the memories from long ago surface. Two eighteen-year-olds in a dorm room at college, kissing passionately, trying to stop ourselves. Finding each other in the dark, over and over again, yet saying nothing in the light of day. Making a decision to accept that it could be right and then knowing for sure why it was terribly, terribly wrong. I've been bearing the burden and living with the punishment ever since. I think about how I spent the next two years in college, and so many after, dutifully dating boys, even taking the pledge of virginity, because it was an easy way out. I've been hoping that as I matured, I'd come around to feeling all the right attractions, instead of the wrong ones. And I still hold that hope. Just because I wasn't attracted to Mike, doesn't mean I won't find a man eventually.

&⮞

When Sunday comes around, I feel a heavy weight of dread settle into my body. I don't want to sit in the pews and watch the service from that angle. I don't want to listen to the choir and not be part of it. I don't want to have to answer questions from other choir members about why I'm not singing. And most of all, I don't want to face Mike. But it's Sunday and I do want to praise the Lord. I could try a different church but I have no idea where I would go. In the end I decide to forego church altogether and take a hike into the foothills.

In summer the hills dry out and get brown, but spring is the perfect time to see the snow melt roaring over the massive granite boulders. I use the switchbacks to climb higher and higher. Golden California poppies and mauve lupines cover the hills. As I climb higher my nostrils are assailed with the fresh scent of Douglas Firs. At the top of the canyon I look down toward the clear, cool river tumbling down the hillside and I stand in awe, marveling at God's glorious creation. A song comes into my head, and

I realize it's the hymn we were practicing for today. I open my mouth and sing out in full voice, my song carrying upwards toward the raptors gliding above me. I feel God's presence all around me, and I feel closer to myself than I have for a very long time.

Clambering over the granite boulders and along the gravel trail, I feel so lucky to be alive. Lizzie used to love this hike. Before she met Kurt, we would challenge each other to find hikes that were ever more demanding. No matter the season, we'd scramble over muddy rocks in winter and hike along dusty paths in summer. We'd climb higher and walk farther, determined to outdo each other, never admitting to sore muscles and blistered feet. I wish I could feel her presence with me now, but all I feel is the absence of it. Which brings me with a thud back to reality.

I need to know what really happened to my sister and I need to bring her justice.

Chapter Nineteen

I spend a few days wallowing in my misery until I remember the reason I was late to choir in the first place: I'd been thinking about JP and Munchausen by proxy and questioning whether Lizzie really had FSGS or if JP somehow caused her symptoms. I need to talk to her doctor or the nurses who attended her at the hospital. Someone has to know or suspect something. If the hospital did anything wrong, they'll want to cover their butts, so they won't be willing to tell me. But what if there was something that could only be known with hindsight?

I don't think I can do this by phone, nor can I have Paula or Cleo take it on. Firstly, they're not family members, and secondly, they don't know about my suspicions regarding JP. What if I took a day off and flew to Philly? But will her doctor be willing to talk to me? I know physicians can't disclose confidential patient information when their patient is still alive. What about after they're gone? Would there be any harm in him discussing Lizzie's situation with me now that she's dead? Just to be sure, I Google the limits of confidentiality. I'm surprised to find out that the medical profession is only allowed to disclose information about a deceased person under very strict conditions. Saying I want to examine my sister's file to see if someone missed something isn't a good enough reason. But physicians *can* break confidentiality if it's to disclose genetic information to at-risk family members who can benefit from the disclosure.

I got tested right after Lizzie called me, but Dr. Marshall doesn't have to know that. What if I said that Lizzie had been very vague with me about her illness and now I'm starting to have some symptoms myself?

Definitely worth a shot.

ॐ

When I disembark the plane in Philadelphia, my whole body starts to shudder. I feel as if it's three months ago: that terrible day when JP picked me up from the airport, and I saw Lizzie for the last time.

I take a shuttle downtown and arrive at Dr. Marshall's office just a few minutes before our scheduled appointment at 10:00 a.m. Dr. Marshall was Lizzie's primary care doctor, the one who eventually gave her the diagnosis, but also the one who missed it for so long. He agreed to the appointment with no hesitation. Has he been waiting all this time for someone to come knocking? Perhaps he knows that Lizzie's case is ripe for a malpractice suit, and he's agreed to meet with me as a way to avoid one.

The sign on the wall says he doesn't have office hours today, and when I open the door, the waiting room is empty. A middle-aged receptionist with oversized, dangling, hoop earrings and a tight afro welcomes me and ushers me into the doctor's office.

Dr. Marshall looks like a big, old, bloodhound with heavyset jowls that gravitate down in folds so that you can barely see his neck. He has a large, triangular nose, and even though he's standing, he lowers his chin so he can look over his bifocals at me. He must be close to retirement age. Perhaps that's why he was willing to see me. A younger doctor, schooled in litigation risks, might have avoided any kind of possible confrontation.

"Thanks for meeting with me."

"I'm so sorry for your loss. Your sister's death was very upsetting to me personally. I felt as if I may have dropped the ball in her case." Wow, this guy is definitely old school. He was clearly in medical school long before they started teaching doctors never to admit to any possible wrongdoing for fear of being sued.

"What do you mean?"

"Lizzie was in my practice for years. I didn't see her often—she was pretty healthy overall and only came to see me if she needed a note for work or if she had a virus or infection. She did have high cholesterol, so I made sure she had regular lab tests. She was young to be on a statin. However that's not unheard of. Because statins can cause liver damage, I was always more focused on her liver function than anything else. A couple of times when she was here, her blood pressure was surprisingly high. I put it down to white-coat syndrome—many patients have high blood pressure when they have medical appointments, because they're nervous."

"What about the blood in the urine?"

"Your sister and I were both in denial. She did mention it, but then she said it could have coincided with the beginning or end of menstruation. I should have done a test anyway, but I didn't."

"So what made you finally diagnose FSGS?"

"She'd done her usual annual blood and urine tests in past years, but we changed labs. This time when the results came back, the abnormal results were highlighted in deep red. I couldn't miss it. And that's when I sent her to the hospital for the FSGS test."

They changed labs and got different results? Is there any way JP could have had some part in that? Could she have somehow had the lab work diverted to her own address? I ask Dr. Marshall about the labs. He says they used to work with a very small local lab, but they switched to a national network. I'm familiar with the name; it's one they have in California too. So it doesn't seem possible that JP could have been involved with any result tampering. Still I want to be sure.

"Maybe they weren't highlighted before that because they weren't abnormal. What made you change labs?"

He shrugs, his jowls quivering as he does so. "I'm just the doctor, my dear." He smiles, a look of irony in his eyes. "You'd have to ask the bureaucrats about that."

Is there any way JP could have influenced that decision? I make a note to ask the assistant who ushered me in here about the lab switch.

"Do you think if you'd diagnosed Lizzie sooner, she wouldn't have deteriorated as quickly?"

"No. If I thought that for a moment, we wouldn't be having this conversation." He smiles a mischievous grin; he's not quite as naïve as I'd thought. He's only talking to me because he's convinced I have no reason to sue. "It wouldn't have made a difference if I'd given her the diagnosis sooner. Her case was fairly mild, so apart from some dietary changes—reducing sodium intake for example—she didn't need any further treatment."

I sit back in my chair. Jet lag is beginning to set in, but I have to stay focused.

"Could it be that you missed her condition because she didn't really have FSGS? That all those years when she had high cholesterol it was just that and nothing more?"

"I wish that were true. But when I reviewed her case, I could see that she'd had all the same symptoms for years."

"May I—may I see her file?" I ask.

He shakes his head. "Patient confidentiality. Why do you want to see it?"

"I want to understand why she had such a sudden deterioration if her case was so mild. It seems to me that either it wasn't so mild after all, or whatever happened to her had nothing to do with FSGS."

"These things happen. I've been in the profession so many years that nothing surprises me anymore. I've had patients I thought were dying make a miraculous recovery and, as in the unfortunate case of your sister, the opposite." He stops, and leans forward across the desk. "I'm so sorry for your loss, my dear, and I hope I've been of some help to you. We doctors like to think we're infallible, but even in these days of advanced science, there's still an awful lot of trial and error. Look at cancer management: Why do some people respond to certain treatment while others receive identical treatment and it doesn't help? Call it providence or Divine Intervention, but the fact is, sometimes, things just happen."

He stands up, indicating that our meeting is over. I like him. He's honest and sincere. Nevertheless, I don't agree with him.

These things don't just happen. Not to Lizzie anyway. There's an explanation, and I'm becoming more and more convinced that it has to do with JP.

My next stop is the hospital. I've asked to meet with the doctor who treated Lizzie in order to discuss my own health concerns. I have an appointment with Dr. Patel.

"I appreciate you seeing me, doctor." His skin is so dark, he must come from the most southern part of India.

"Let me say first of all, I'm so sorry for your loss. Were you very close to her?"

"Yes. Especially after our parents died. For a while we clung to each other, until she moved on and met her spouse."

"May I ask how your parents died? Was it related in any way to this medical issue?" His head bobs from one shoulder to the other as he talks. He has a little goatee that he strokes lovingly. His startlingly blue eyes look kind.

"Oh, no. They were killed in a car crash. We donated their organs, and I've always assumed that if anything abnormal had been found, someone would have notified us."

Dr. Patel nods. "The note in the file stated that you were at your sister's side when she died."

"Yes. JP called me the day before. It was the first I knew how seriously ill she was. I jumped on a plane right away, and I thank the Lord every day that I got here in time."

He places his hand on his heart then puts his two hands together in the sign of prayer.

"Tell me how I can help you."

"I know Lizzie had FSGS. I didn't really think about it until a couple of weeks ago when my doctor told me I had high cholesterol and high blood pressure. I was surprised, and all of a sudden, I had this horrible feeling that perhaps I have what Lizzie had."

"Your doctor should be able to do a series of tests to determine that."

"Yes, he will. My concern is how quickly Lizzie died. It seemed as if one day she was healthy and the next day she was gone."

He strokes his goatee, pulling it down in a rhythm that's almost meditative. "After you called, I went into our electronic medical records and looked over your sister's case to familiarize myself with it."

"You weren't the doctor who treated her?"

"We're a teaching hospital. Our residents rotate throughout the various departments and then move on to

other medical centers. In your sister's case, not only did
the resident move across the country but the Attending
took up a better position elsewhere too."
Damn. Dr. Patel never even met my sister.
"Once you looked at the record, what did you think?"
"Her case was highly unusual."
"Oh?" I feign surprise.
"Her kidneys seemed to stop working all of a sudden,
which is not what we expect with FSGS."
"So how do you explain that?"
"I'm not sure that I can."
"Really?"
He smiles. "We doctors aren't omnipotent, you know.
Even if we sometimes act like we are."
I pause, wondering whether I can ask the burning
question that has been smoldering in my brain for weeks
now. I don't want to alienate the doctor by sounding crazy.
I feel a dull thudding in my chest as my pulse starts to
race. "Could someone have done anything to induce my
sister's kidney failure?"
Dr. Patel stares at me for a moment. Did I go too far?
Now that it's out, I plow on. "Is there anything about my
sister's symptoms that would have made you question her
diagnosis if you hadn't already known it?"
Dr. Patel strokes his goatee and his eyes squint
together.
"I don't think so," he says. I catch a hesitation, as if
there is something he's not willing to say.
"You're not positive."
He hesitates again then says, "Is there any possibility
that your sister may have tried to kill herself?"
It's not what I expected to hear.
"No!" I bang my glass on the table so hard that liquid
spills out of it. Then I remember the notecard. "I don't
think so. Why do you ask?"
He shakes his head. "It's nothing. Forget it."
"I need answers," I say softly. "I'm not looking to sue
the hospital or anything like that. I just need answers
about my sister."
He stands up, walks over to the office window, and
stares out.
I get up and stand next to him. "Please?"

He looks at me, his eyes full of sympathy, then shakes his head.

"Really," he says, "it's nothing."

His cell phone buzzes and he looks down. "I'm being paged. I have to go. I don't think I can help you. I have your phone number. If I think of anything, I'll call you."

He walks me to the door of his office and we step into the hall together. He turns to me and puts his hand out.

"Good luck," he says and marches quickly down the corridor, pulling his arms into the sleeves of his white coat before he disappears around the corner.

Frustrated, I walk slowly down the hall, trying to figure out what I said that triggered an idea for him.

Because although he denied it, he's on to something, I'm sure of it.

Chapter Twenty

The email from Luke is a terse one: I'm to meet him in his office the moment I get to school. He's been so supportive of me since Lizzie died that I'm surprised, until I remember that he did this once before and it had nothing to do with me directly. A newspaper had discovered we expelled a pregnant student. Their readers were shocked by the policy, and by the fact that all students sign a pledge regarding the consequences of sexual immorality. The newspaper's angle was that it was sexist, since the girl who got pregnant was expelled, but the unknown boy who impregnated her wasn't. Luke asked me to handle the phone calls and letters that ensued. I wonder if Luke's calling me in about something similar today.

When I open the door, Luke is alone in his office. He beckons me to sit, and a moment later, Matthew, the school attorney walks in. He sits next to Luke, across from me, pulls out a folder, and holds it in front of him.

"There's no easy way to say this, Ashley, so I'll get right to it." Luke looks embarrassed and I suddenly get an inkling that this meeting may not be good news. "We have to let you go."

I'm stunned. This is coming out of nowhere. "Why?" I try not to sound belligerent.

"We're not satisfied with your work."

"Not satisfied? But I got us Good News gospel choir. And last year's evaluation said I was an outstanding employee. What's changed?"

"We have reason to believe you've been encouraging the kids into immoral behavior."

"Me? Immoral...?" My heart is racing furiously. What

could I possibly have done?

Matthew, the attorney, leans forward in his chair and says, "Please read this to me."

"Grace Covenant School reserves the right, within its sole discretion, to refuse admission of an applicant and/or to discontinue enrollment of a student participating in, promoting, supporting or condoning pornography, sexual immorality, homosexual activity or bisexual activity, or displaying an inability or resistance to support the qualities and characteristics required of a biblically based and Christ-like lifestyle." I look up at Matthew. "It's the pledge our students sign. What does this have to do with me?"

He pulls another piece of paper out from the file. "Now read this."

"Christian counselors do not condone or advocate for the pursuit of or active involvement in homosexual, bisexual or transgendered behaviors and lifestyles. Counselors may agree to and support the desire to work through issues of homosexual and transgendered identity and attractions, but will encourage sexual celibacy or biblically-prescribed sexual behavior while such issues are being addressed."

"Do you know what that is?" Matthew asks.

"It's self-explanatory. It's how Christian counselors are meant to deal with gay kids." As I say it, my heart sinks and I have an awful feeling I know what's coming.

"You signed this agreement, which states that you would not condone homosexual behavior and would encourage sexual celibacy. You are aware, I believe, that Jordan Sterling is in an intimate relationship with another boy?"

"I'm not sure that they're intimate. I didn't ask for details."

"Let me assure you that there is proof that he is in a relationship that is an abomination. Apparently, you do not hold the same beliefs."

"I—I didn't encourage him. I didn't advocate anything."

"You knew about it but you told him not to tell his parents. That sounds like you were condoning his behavior and encouraging him to get away with it."

"No. I told him not to tell them because I thought

it might just be a phase."

For the first time Luke looks up and faces me directly. "I'm so disappointed in you, Ashley."

"Come on, Luke, you know what half these boys do when they're in the restrooms and they don't grow up gay. I just thought—"

Matthew puts up his hand in a halt sign. "I've heard quite enough. I can't believe you've been a part of this school and our church for so long when you hold these heretical views."

They're firing me. I'm not being let go, I'm being expelled, just like the pregnant teenager.

"What's going to happen to Jordan? Are you going to expel him?"

"No decision has been made." I'm surprised. Why would they consider keeping him? Then I remember that his parents are major donors. So I will be the sacrificial lamb on the altar of donor parents, who will be pleased to know that the problem isn't their child, it's the boy next door and the school staff member who didn't try to stop it.

"How do you know that Jordan and I talked?"

"Because when his mother walked in on them *in flagrante delicto* the first thing out of his mouth was, 'I wanted to tell you, but Miss Glynn said not to.'"

I am well and truly sunk.

"We're not completely heartless, Ashley," Luke says, although he still won't look me in the eyes. "We've arranged for you to get three months' severance."

"We just need you to sign these papers," Matthew says, handing them to me.

"What are they?"

"Forms that state you're resigning of your own free will and—"

"But I'm not resigning. You're firing me."

"No. If you don't sign the papers, we'll fire you. If you do, your personnel record will show that you resigned. Which for your future career will be an extremely important difference."

Matthew hands me the papers and I start to read them. It looks like legalese. Buried in the middle is a phrase about nondisclosure regarding the conditions of my departure.

"What does this part mean?"

"It means we're going to give you severance. In return you're not going to try to sue us or discuss the terms of this agreement. Disclosure to the media would result in immediate action against you."

"The media...? Is this termination legal?"

"Absolutely. Private schools don't have the same restrictions public schools do. You know that." He's right and I've always supported it. I wouldn't have joined Grace Covenant if I didn't believe in the Christian values of the school. But maybe without realizing it, I've started to move away from some of those beliefs. And maybe Lizzie's death, and being around so many of her wonderful friends, has really put me on a divergent path from my church.

"How long do I have to wind down? I need to finalize the concert details with the choir, and I'm halfway through a big grant proposal. I could probably get everything done in a week."

Luke's head is back to facing the floor and it's left to Matthew to say, "We need you to sign the papers, gather up your stuff, and say your goodbyes. From previous experience, we've discovered that's the best way to do it."

My head is reeling. This morning I came into work a long-standing, valuable employee and now I'm nothing? I'm mad at myself for not realizing what I was doing when I spoke with Jordan. And I'm mad at an institution that would put aside all the good work I've done and sacrifice me to the demands of an outraged parent. I don't want to sign the form, but the severance pay will be extremely helpful. If they fire me, I won't even be able to collect unemployment. And I know Matthew is right: even though the progressive media might be outraged that I could be pushed out over supporting a gay student, legally Grace Covenant does have the right to push me out the door.

I pick up the pen. "Where do I sign?"

Chapter Twenty-One

It's downright peculiar to be at home on a workday with no plans, and even stranger to think that I now have no church home. I should feel angry, but instead, I feel strangely liberated. Grace Covenant was my rock for so long. It's been crumbling for a while, and now it's washed away altogether. I'll miss the kids, just as I already miss singing in the choir, but I'm ready to start a new chapter in my life. I can find a new church home. I'll research local houses of worship. Come to that, there's no reason for me to stay where I am. I could move away altogether.

I spend the morning scrubbing down the kitchen, a chore I've put off for a rainy day, even though the sun is shining and it's warm and bright outside. I feel as if I'm performing a thorough cleansing, not just of my kitchen, but of my life as I've known it. As I throw away grungy spray bottles, I contemplate whether it really is time to relocate. But where? The obvious place might be Philadelphia, now that I have some new friends there. What would it be like to depend on a group of women who live a lifestyle so different from mine? If I were in Philly, JP and I could find out the truth about Lizzie's death. I still don't understand why she was so reticent when I tried to tell her what Lizzie said. Maybe she couldn't bear the thought of what might have happened. Yet surely on some level she must want to know too. I have so many questions that only she can answer.

After Lizzie died, I made a note on my phone of everything I could remember about that last morning with her. I wrote down the words she said, even though it didn't make sense. While I wait for the floor to dry, I take another look at what I wrote and notice two questions I keyed in, beneath the words: Why didn't the hospital run a tox screen on Lizzie, and why didn't they insist on an autopsy? I have to talk to JP. I call her cell phone but it goes through to voicemail. I leave a message telling her something urgent has come up in hopes of enticing her to answer. When she hasn't responded an hour later, I compose an email, even though she doesn't like them. I make it brief, then click Send. A moment later a message pops up on my laptop: undeliverable, addressee unknown. That's weird. I wait a couple of hours and call her cell phone again. This time I get a canned message telling me that the number I'm dialing is no longer in service. An uncomfortable feeling stirs in my stomach, a mix of nausea and fear. Why would JP cut herself off from me?

I call Paula and ask her if she's heard from JP lately.

She laughs. "If I waited for a call from JP, I might sooner see Haley's comet next time around."

I tell her what happened when I tried to call. She tells me she has a second number for JP and puts me on hold while she dials it. Moments later she's back with me and says that number's no longer in service either.

"Would you be willing to go round there and see what's going on?" I ask.

She agrees to do so and promises to call me back.

I pace up and down in my apartment. There's something really fishy going on and I don't like the smell of it.

I think back to that Sunday evening with JP when I told her about Lizzie's last words. She was angry with me for suggesting there was any truth to them. She insisted that Lizzie was doped up. She didn't want to entertain the idea that anything Lizzie said was true. As I replay the scene in my head, I become aware of something strange, something I never noticed before. When I told her about the idea of poison, she was angry, *but she didn't seem surprised.*

An idea starts to form in my head, a very unpleasant idea.

I pick up the phone and frantically punch in Helen's phone number. When she answers, I jump right in, no pleasantries, no explanation.

"You said Lizzie was at the gym the same day she

was admitted to the hospital. I thought you meant earlier in the day, but now I'm starting to wonder. What time did you see her there?"

"I was doing my spinning class which runs from 6-7:30 p.m. We were in the changing room together afterward. She was gussying up in a cocktail dress and heels. They were going out to some swanky restaurant for dinner. Why, what's the matter?"

I ignore her question. "And JP was there?"

"She'd just finished her swim. She was getting dressed too, though not as fancy as Lizzie. Black jeans and a pressed shirt. I don't know which restaurant they were at when Lizzie collapsed."

"Restaurant?"

"Isn't that what happened? JP told us she and Lizzie went out to a restaurant, and Lizzie collapsed."

"Did they call an ambulance?"

"No. JP insisted it was better for her to take Lizzie to the hospital because the ambulance would be required to take her to the closest one and she wanted to take Lizzie where they were already familiar with her case."

I'm trying to think, but my head feels all jumbled up. JP told her friends that Lizzie collapsed. She never mentioned anything about her being drunk. And yet, by the time they got to the hospital Lizzie was intoxicated. Something here doesn't add up.

I make my excuses to get off the phone, then pace some more, unable to think straight, unable to do anything until I hear from Paula.

When the phone rings, my hands are shaking so badly I almost drop it.

"I'm at JP's. Her truck's not here and there are no lights on in the house. Maybe she's gone away for a few days."

Maybe she has, but I have a bad feeling in the pit of my stomach that it's more than that.

"Can you go around the back and make sure everything's okay?"

"I can do better than that. Years ago, Lizzie gave me a spare key in case they ever got locked out. I'm not sure JP even knows I have one. Hold on a minute, while I fish it out and open the front door."

I hear the sounds of fumbling, then Paula murmurs to herself. "Here it is."

Sounds like she has to make an effort to fit it into the lock. Perhaps age has rusted the key, or the weather has warped the cylinder. She grunts with the effort of trying to get it to turn, and then all of a sudden I hear a click and the sound of the door being pushed open.

My heart stands still, yet I'm surprisingly calm when Paula exclaims in a gasp, "It's empty, Ash. The house is completely empty."

It's all starting to come together. *Why was I so stupid?* Why did it take me so long to figure it out? Lizzie told me everything I needed to know. I just didn't put it together. Lizzie wasn't telling me her lover had poisoned her. She was telling me loud and clear who did it, and I was too oblivious to notice.

And now that I know, it may be too late. JP's gone. She must have got scared when I told her about Lizzie's last words. She knew it was only a matter of time before I stumbled on the truth.

I have to find JP. She's been smart, but I'm going to have to be smarter. She's been one step ahead—or maybe several steps ahead—of all of us. But that's going to change. Because I will track her down, and when I do, I will do everything in my power to bring her to justice.

PART TWO

JP

Chapter Twenty-Two

The Year Before Lizzie Died

It's 5:00 a.m. when I finally hear Lizzie turn her key in the lock and try to open the front door. She can't, of course, because I've put the deadbolt on. Did she really think she could sneak back in, creep up the stairs, and pretend she'd been home for hours? Once I realized she wasn't coming home last night, I slid the deadbolt; I wanted to make sure that in case I dropped off, I wouldn't miss "welcoming" her home. I couldn't sleep. I sat in the rocker, glided back and forth, and held my hand on my betrayed heart. I imagined how it had been soft, pink and expansive, and now it was turning red and hard and shriveling up. I could see it in my mind's eye, cracking and splintering.

Lizzie jiggles her key in the lock and rattles the door a few more times, while I start to imagine what's running through her head. Is she beginning to panic? Is the adrenaline coursing through her veins as she realizes that I may be waiting on the other side of the door? Is fear quickening her pulse and making her heart hammer? Let it. I have all the power now. I could decide not to let her in at all. How long will she stand on the doorstep, shivering in the early morning chill? I don't know what she was wearing when she left yesterday, but I'm pretty sure she was ill prepared for the cold air that moved in and made the temperature plummet. Is she stomping her feet, wrapping her arms around herself, wondering why the door won't open? Or does she know perfectly well? Is she preparing what she's going to say, what kind of excuses she's going to make? Suddenly I can't stand it anymore and as she turns the key, I pull back the deadbolt. She tumbles over the threshold and almost falls into my arms. I step nimbly out of the way. I don't want to even touch her traitorous skin.

"What the—?" She cries out a little, falls forward, and puts out her hand to stop herself. Her snappy, leather purse goes flying in front of her and she lands on her knees, banging them on the hardwood floor, as she ends up splayed in front of me. For a moment she looks like a penitent who has flung herself at the feet of a priest, asking for forgiveness.

"For God's sake, get up." I turn away and walk down the hall.

She gathers herself and comes tripping after me. "JP, I can explain..."

"Oh yes," I tell her, "you certainly can. And you will. Right now." And then, before I can stop myself, I raise my arm, pull it back, and swing it, the palm of my hand open, intending to give her a sharp slap across the face. She jerks her head back. I end up cuffing her ear and she stumbles for a moment. She looks at me in shock, and I know we are both thinking the same thing: she once told me if I ever hit her, she'd walk out. Well, go ahead. Go right ahead.

"I'm sorry," she says, lowering her gaze to the floor. She raises it and looks me in the eyes. "I should have called."

"I got scared," she says later, "when the doctor started talking about a kidney transplant."

We're sitting in the kitchen drinking strong cups of coffee. Lizzie's ear is bright red, and I'm starting to feel remorse for having hit her. Her eyes are bloodshot, which can only mean one thing. Hopefully, the coffee will help the   hangover.

"I was afraid," she says.

"So you went out and got drunk."

"Yes—no. I mean...it wasn't like that."

"Someone else poured alcohol down your gullet?" My temper starts to flare again. I may have promised to never hit her, but equally, she promised me she'd never drink. So this kinda makes us even.

"I was feeling upset. The diagnosis sounds so serious. I mean...a kidney transplant?"

"He said it could be way down the line, if things get bad."

"I know. But all I could think of was how my health is just going to keep on deteriorating."

Even though I'm mad, I do feel sorry for her. I don't know what it's like to be handed a serious diagnosis, and I hope I never will. "That was a good reason to go out and get drunk?"

Lizzie's been sober for nine years. When we first met, she used to go to AA regularly. Last year she decided she didn't need it any more. I was torn when she told me that. I couldn't stand all that Higher Power mumbo-jumbo and was happy for her to drop that side of things. On the other hand, I wondered what would happen if she ever had a crisis. Now I know the answer.

"There's never a good reason to drink, I know that. But I wasn't exactly thinking straight." Lizzie rubs her eyes, making them even redder than they already are.

"Why didn't you tell me how you were feeling? I'm your wife, I'm the one you're meant to talk to." My coffee is too strong and I add some half-and-half. Lizzie takes a small sip from her mug.

"Because all I could think about was that sooner or later I'm going to end up being a burden to you. When things get worse, you're the one who's going to have to take care of me. I couldn't imagine how you felt about that. You've been acting like it's not such a big deal, so I didn't see any point in getting you all worked up about it too."

"I wouldn't have got worked up. The doctor said it's different for everyone. Yes, he mentioned kidney transplants. He also mentioned people who respond to treatment, people who live for years without any major symptoms. Why are you so convinced you'll be one of the worst-case scenarios, instead of one of the patients who can easily keep it under control?"

"I guess it's all so new to me. One day I think I'm just a normal woman with nothing wrong with me, and the next, I have a chronic disease."

"You thought I couldn't handle that? That I'd leave you because you were sick?"

Lizzie has only the vaguest idea of my history. But even with what I've shared, doesn't she know I would never, ever walk out?

"No. I know you'd be there for me. It's me. I don't know if *I* can handle it. It's like living with a death sentence hanging over me. Not knowing when the ax is going to fall. Perhaps I drank because I knew it would make matters worse. Maybe I just wanted to speed it up."

My coffee tastes bitter in my mouth. Or maybe the bitterness is knowing Lizzie stayed out all night. I go over to the sink and throw the dregs away.

"You told me you were going to Paula's, to hang out. Were you lying about that?"

"Not originally. Then I read about a girl band playing at The Dykery up in New Hope. It sounded like something I'd have gone to years ago, and I wanted to feel young and normal again."

And single. She doesn't say it, but the implication is clear. So while I sat at home, watching *Mad Men* reruns, she was living it up at a gay bar.

"I saw this woman I used to know from before you and I met. She invited me to sit with her and her friends. One of them bought a round of drinks. I should have said something, but all I could think was, I may die soon and I want to have another drink before I do. I figured I'd just have one."

"Jeez, Lizzie. You were in AA for long enough to know you can't have just one."

"Some people can. I thought, why can't I be like them, just nurse a gin and tonic for the evening?"

I shake my head. If there's one thing I've never understood about alcoholics, it's how they manage to kid themselves, over and over. They all think they can be a "normie" despite all proof to the contrary. Except that I thought Lizzie was different. I thought she really got it.

"Then what happened?"

"People started dancing to the band. I guess while I was on the floor, someone bought another round..."

"Didn't your 'friend' try to stop you?"

"She—she went home early. Said she could feel a migraine coming on. She tried to get me to leave with her, but I didn't want to. It was so great to be dancing, drinking, living it up like the old days. I told her I was fine and that she should go. One of the women said they'd give me a ride home."

I feel my chest tighten.

"But the ride she gave you wasn't just in her car." My voice sounds like a sheet of steel, flat and gray.

I wait for her to reassure me: *Oh, no, it wasn't like that.* She doesn't.

"Who was it?" The steel has turned into a knife, cutting through the air, piercing my heart.

"You don't know her." There is a silence. Lizzie stares at her empty coffee cup and I wonder whether I want to hear the details. I decide that I don't.

"It won't happen again," she whispers, "I promise."

"Getting drunk? Or sleeping with a stranger?" My eyes narrow as I glare at her.

"Both." She tries to look me in the eyes but ends up lowering her head.

ॐ

For days after Lizzie admits to the affair, I'm devastated. She swears up, down and sideways that it was just a one-night stand. "Why do you keep calling it an affair?" she asks, as if the idea that giving away her married body for one night versus several is perfectly acceptable. She keeps reiterating that she was upset about the diagnosis, that she went to the bar in a moment of weakness. She swears she'll never drink again. She promises she'll always be faithful, that she loves me and it didn't mean anything. I guess she should have thought about that before she took off her pants for a woman who wasn't her wife.

I think about finding the bitch she screwed and doing some serious damage to her. Part of me wants to see how Lizzie would react; would it hurt her to see her fuck-buddy harmed? But if something happened to that woman, Lizzie will know it was me, and might feel morally obligated to report it to someone, like law enforcement. That's the kind of value system she apparently has: betray your wife; act with integrity the rest of the time. I decide not to mess with whoever it was. I know if I do something to someone else, it won't help me. It's Lizzie I'll never be able to trust again, Lizzie I can't live with after what she's done. She's ruined everything. We had the perfect life—well, OK, not quite so perfect, but pretty damn good—and with one stupid night, she's wrecked it.

After several days of me giving her the silent treatment, she asks if I want a divorce. "Why?" I want to ask. "So you can go back to the bar bimbo?" I'm not about to let her off that easily. In addition, I can't stand the thought that she'll be out there, getting on with her life, while mine is ruined. So no, Lizzie, no divorce.

I think about forgiving her. But it's not an option. All I have to do is remember Mom: *I won't drink anymore, I promise. I'll never leave you again.*

I've heard it all before. I won't live through it another time. No one's going to make a fool out of me, ever again.

So instead of forgiving, I do a lot of research and make my plan.

Once I know what I'm going to do, I stop the silent treatment. I tell her how much I love her (which is true) and that I forgive her (which isn't). We have the best make-up sex we've had in years. I tell her we're never going to mention the incident again. And I never do. I think she's surprised I don't go on some kind of furious rampage. But I don't need to get mad.

I'm going to get even.

Chapter Twenty-Three

I decide to give us a year. Knowing that my time with her is limited, I fall in love with her even more deeply than ever. That year turns out to be the best of our entire relationship. We are so close, so loving. I stop being jealous of all the time she spends with her book group and her library buddies. In fact, I encourage her to go out with them, to enjoy their company. Let them feel her loss as much as I will after it's over. On our anniversary, I buy her a dozen red roses, and when she thanks me for them, I cry, knowing they will be the last flowers I ever give her.

She brushes my tears away with her sleeve. "You're too good to me," she says in a choked voice. "I don't deserve it."

"I love you Lizzie, I'll never stop loving you," I tell her, and it's true. Just because you plan to kill someone, it doesn't mean you don't love them.

I hope I never again have to endure the pain of those last days when she is in the E.R. Knowing you're going to lose the only person you have ever loved totally and completely, is intolerable. I feel as if a massive weight is sitting on my chest, and the knife that is now lodged permanently in my heart twists deeper. My sympathy goes out to Lizzie, who looks awful, bloated and hooked up to the machines. While she can still talk, she keeps apologizing to me for getting sick.

"Don't be silly," I tell her, "it's not your fault. Some things are beyond your control."

I squeeze her bloated hand and stroke the silky, chestnut hair I love so much. I feel it against my fingers, and the pain of knowing I'll never stroke it again is almost unbearable. I stay strong in her presence, but that first night when she's in the E.R., I come home and fall sobbing onto our bed, clawing at the quilt, knowing she'll never sleep under it again, inhaling the musky scent of her that still lingers on the sheets.

Did Lizzie know she had killed herself the moment she opened her legs to the woman who took her home that night? When did she start to put together what really happened to her? Was it while I stroked her hand and told her how much I loved her? Or was it that same night I came home and clawed the bed sheets? While I drank in the last remnants of her scent, did she lie in her hospital bed and work out the details?

If I had any idea she figured it out, I never would have given Ash time alone with her. But she never gave any indication. How much effort it must have taken, to let me touch her and whisper words of love, once she knew it was me. Thank God when she had her chance, she couldn't make Ash understand. Of course not. Dear, naïve Ashley.

Dear, my ass.

Ash was never dear to me, although I probably fooled her into thinking she was. She and Lizzie were both alike when it came to believing that forgiveness can come so easily. I never forgot that crass, stupid remark Ash made the first time we met: "Oh, I didn't know Lizzie had a boyfriend." Did she think that was something I would just put out of my mind? Did she think her simple little apology made it all okay? There are some things you don't forget or forgive.

I guess I should count myself lucky. "She kept asking for you," Ash says when she finally divulges Lizzie's last words. I don't think so. Lizzie was trying so hard to tell her what I did, but Ash was too naïve to comprehend.

When Ash brings up the word "poison," I'll admit I get nervous. On the one hand, if she thinks some ex-lover did it, that's great. But if she starts delving into the idea that someone poisoned Lizzie, it can only mean trouble. So I head her off at the pass, and she accepts it.

I'm nervous but not overly scared. It's not as if she could do anything, even if she does figure it all out. Ash has no idea that she was the one who helped me dispose of the remaining proof.

After she leaves, I start thinking. What if she keeps calling and asking me for more and more information? I can't risk it. If I change my number but stick around, Paula and her friends will easily track me down for her.

I'd already been contemplating selling the house and moving on, and after Ash starts probing, I know for sure.

It's time to get out of Dodge.

Chapter Twenty-Four

When I contact a realtor, I'm shocked by how much he says I can get for the property. Apparently, the improvements Lizzie and I made increased the value dramatically. I tell him I don't want any signs outside the house, and I don't need to get the highest price. If he can find a cash buyer, I'll lower the price even more. The house sells in two days. After the mortgage is paid off, I have enough money to buy a motorhome, pay the extras associated with it—rental space, gas and maintenance—and still have money left to put in the bank. I scan Craigslist and am rewarded when I find somebody selling a barely used, 19-foot, state-of-the-art Roadtrek RV.

The moment I see it, I love it. It reminds me of the first studio apartment I lived in after I graduated from college. It has everything you need in the tiniest space possible. It has a fully equipped kitchen; the driver's cab doubles as a living room; there's a dining area that I can use as an office; and I can keep the bed single or open it into a double. Most important, there's a toilet and shower, so I won't be roughing it. I don't even try to negotiate with the owner, just ask him to show me how everything works, before I hand over a cashier's check.

I pack up as quickly as possible.

There's so little space that almost everything has to go. Up until now, I've left Lizzie's wardrobe untouched. Now I dive in and grab handfuls of sweaters and tops, trying not to inhale the scent of her which lingers on everything. I pull her blouses, dresses and pants off hangers and fling them into boxes. I throw out all her underwear and leggings, and even though I want to keep her favorite rainbow wool socks, I force myself to ditch them too. I run a quick hand over all the shelves and make sure the closet is bare. Next I pack boxes full of all her books and music. I make numerous runs to the charity stores and thrift shops, and when all the boxes are gone, I breathe a sigh of relief and move on to the easier task of deciding how much of my own stuff I have room for.

It takes me almost a day to pack the Roadtrek and arrange the closet spaces so that every inch is used effectively. I consider making a complete break by leaving Lizzie's ashes behind, but I can't force myself. I keep a single photograph and put it inside one of the little cabinets with the urn. The next morning I take my pickup truck to a dealer who's promised me a couple of thousand for it. He drives me back home, although I don't think of it as home any more. It's just an empty house that I once lived in. Uhura, as I've decided to name the Roadtrek, sits waiting for me, and with relief, I jump in and pull out of the driveway for the last time.

As I make my way down Route 76 I try to ignore Kelly Drive and Boathouse Row so I won't remember the picnics, the walks, the bicycle rides we took along the river. Those were truly the happiest days of my life. But they're gone now. I have to look forward not back. I feel light and unencumbered. Tomorrow will be a new morning.

At first, it's quite an adjustment, living in a 21-foot, narrow van after owning a rambling 2,000-square-foot, two-story house. Everything is so compact that I can go from kitchen to office, bedroom to bathroom in a few steps. I never realized how much exercise I got when I walked up the garden path to the house, paced the hallway through to the living room, climbed up and down the stairs, or made my way into the backyard. Now each time I stop for fuel, I walk around the gas station just to stretch my legs, and wherever I park for the night, I take a long walk around the perimeter of the campground.

The first night I pull into a state park in the wooded Pine Barons of New Jersey. I sign up just for one night, but it's so quiet and peaceful, I end up staying for a week. I get up each morning, do my editing work, and wander down paths that I have entirely to myself. Once I even take my shirt off and walk half-naked in nature, my mind wandering with me. I don't think about the past—what's done is done—but I try to imagine my future. I'm faced with a blank screen. It's unnerving and I don't try it again.

After a week I head out to the famed Assateague Island in Virginia, where the wild ponies roam free. "Would you like to pay for just one night at a time?" the park ranger asks. "Most people do."

It seems strange, until I discover the biting horse flies, so vicious I can't move without getting bitten. I get the hell out of there and never do see the wild ponies.

My next stop is Amicalola Falls State Park in Georgia, because I edited an article about it once and it sounded beautiful. It's too far to drive in one day, so I make a stop at a commercial RV park on the way. I'm shocked by how different it is from the state parks. It's twice the price and the only thing it has going for it is Wi-Fi. The RVs are all lined up next to each other, and if I don't draw my curtains, my neighbors can see everything I do. I beat a hasty retreat the next morning and by mid-afternoon I pull into Amicalola and make my way down an extremely steep hill to the small campground. After I hook Uhura up, I set out in search of one of the many hiking trails I've read about. I'm barely past the first row of campsites when I spot several women sitting on camping chairs in a circle. I don't need gaydar to tell me there isn't a straight one among them.

"Hi," a woman wearing a Florida Marlins ball cap calls. "Want to join us?" The woman pulls out an extra chair, places it next to her, and I lower myself into it. A large woman with breasts that seem to float around her waist tears the cardboard off a six-pack and goes to hand me a beer, but I shake my head. She shrugs and pulls the tab off the can for herself.

"Where you headed?" she asks.

"Traveling around. No particular goal. I just pick a state park and head toward it. If I like it, I stay. If not, I move on."

"Sounds cool. We're headed down to Amelia Island in Florida soon. We'll stay there a couple of weeks, so maybe you'll join us?"

"Maybe. Is it like this?" I indicate the spectacular mountain scenery surrounding us.

"About as different as you can get. Beautiful, but in a totally different, flat kinda way. Guess you're not familiar with the south."

I shake my head. "Where y'all from?"

They laugh. I guess my southern accent doesn't quite work.

"Fort Lauderdale," replies a blonde woman, whose long legs are tanned the purest bronze, and whose breasts look like they may or may not be real. "It's a great place for gay women. Ever thought about living there?" She moves her chair closer to mine.

"Nah. Too big, too crowded, from what I've heard. I want some place smaller but still gay-friendly."

Bronzie pouts her Botox-filled lips a little, but Marlins baseball cap says, "You should check out Tampa Bay. I was in St. Pete last year and met some women from a little town that's just filled with lesbians."

I grin. "Sounds good."

Bronzie turns her face toward me and says, "I take it you're single?"

"Watch out for Darlene," the Marlins ball cap says. "If she sets her sights on you, you're toast."

"Is she the marmalade?" I ask and everyone laughs.

Turns out she is marmalade, jam and honey all rolled into one, and rolling is the operative word. We do plenty of it over the next two days. I think it might be hard, her being my first after Lizzie, but it turns out she's the perfect transitional object. I have absolutely no feelings toward her, but my body performs its mechanical functions just the way it's supposed to. We have two days and screw ourselves stupid, until they leave for Florida. It's just the right amount of time because Bronzie is starting to work my nerves. I still don't know if her breasts are real, and I also don't know anything about her. She has absolutely no conversation beyond Botox and baseball. It makes me miss Lizzie even more, her book-talk and her travel-talk and all the other stuff we used to share together.

"Promise you'll follow us to Amelia Island?" Bronzie sticks her head out of the passenger side of a large Dodge pickup truck, as the group sets off down the hill. She shoves a piece of paper with her phone number into my hand.

"Of course," I say, knowing I won't.

That other place they mentioned, the little town with all the dykes? Now *that* sounds interesting.

Chapter Twenty-Five

The hiking trails in Amicalola are great, and the peace that descends at nightfall is spectacular. I would stay longer if I could, but the rangers told me when I arrived that my site was only available for a few days, so when they're up it's time to leave. I pull out of Amicalola as dawn breaks, so that I can avoid traffic. Eight hours later I pull into Hillsborough River State Park, which has great reviews and is close to Tampa. The ranger directs me to my campsite. Before I head there I ask him about hiking. I also ask whether it's about to pour, because there are ominous clouds overhead.

"Weather forecast said 50-50 chance of rain. At this time of year, that's pretty much what they say every day: hot, humid, and a fifty percent chance of showers."

I'm glad I have Uhura and not one of those poky little tents scattered throughout the campground. I'll risk doing a hike because it's been a long drive. I douse myself in DEET insect repellent and head out onto the trail along the river.

As I make my way along the damp path by the river, the spiky fronds from the Sabal palms fan me, as if I were an Egyptian princess being cooled by servile courtiers. Almost as soon as I start walking, I hear a splash and as I round the   corner, two eyes peer up at me from the water. The gator stares lazily at me, and I sneak by without stopping.

A couple approach wearing matching T-shirts that display proudly they're hiking for Jesus. I have no idea what that means. It reminds me of Ashley. For the first couple of weeks on the road I felt liberated, but recently doubts have started to creep in. I keep wondering if I should have done more to cover my tracks, or better yet, throw anyone who might look for me off the scent with some cockamamie story about Alaska or Hawaii. I'm sure Paula will tell everyone I just need some alone time, but what if Ash continues to ask her pesky questions? What if one day she puts it all together, just like her beautiful, traitorous sister did?

I pull my mind away from thinking about the past and focus instead on the hot breeze that plays around my face. The path splits into two, and just as I'm wondering which fork I should take, I hear footsteps behind me and turn to see another hiker on the path.

"Do you—?"

"Sshh," she whispers, putting her finger to her lips. With her other hand, she points to a deer foraging between the trees.

"Sorry," I mouth, and we stand in silence until the deer darts off in the other direction.

"Hi." This time she speaks out loud. "Sorry if I was rude."

"No worries."

She smiles at me, a smile that's bright and warm, as if she herself is one of those hot Florida rays of sunshine that has emerged from behind the clouds. She's wearing a baseball cap, and from beneath it, auburn wavy hair spills onto her face. Her emerald green eyes draw me in, and when she raises an eyebrow, I realize I've been staring so hard that I forgot to keep the conversation going.

"You were going to ask me something?"

"It's my first time on the trail, and it looks like there are a couple of different options. I was going to ask if you knew the difference." Her khaki cargo shorts reveal tanned, muscled legs and her close-fitting tank top bears a faded rainbow with the slogan, "Out and Proud." A sister, I think and grin inwardly. Too bad I didn't shower and change before I hit the trail. I hope I don't smell like sweat.

"Nice shirt," I say.

She smiles. "This shirt's almost as old as I am, but you know how it is..."

"Absolutely. I have a shirt from the 2000 World Pride a friend brought back from Rome. I've worn it so often it's gray with age."

She holds out her hand. "Katya. My friends call me Kat."

"JP."

A large butterfly alights on a leaf behind her. As I take her hand in mine, my stomach flutters in time with the monarch's vibrating wings. "You're welcome to walk with me," she says. For a moment she looks as if she regrets issuing the invitation, as if she had a plan to walk by herself and maybe I interrupted it.

She's wearing sturdy hiking boots and has no problem with the muddy paths, but when we come to a large puddle, she looks at my sneakers and says, "Change of plan." We turn back to the river and start to follow it downstream. An old wooden bridge spanning the river looms into view.

"A suspension bridge?" I try to keep the anxiety out of my voice.

"Don't worry, it only bounces a little bit." She runs ahead to show me. I hesitate. I hate the idea of going on a hanging bridge, but I don't want to look feeble. I walk across gingerly, trying to make it look as if my lack of speed is so that I can look down-river at the magnificent live oaks and the green, lichen-covered tangles of branches and roots that line the river.

"Obviously, the answer is yes," I say when I finally catch up.

She gives me a puzzled look.

"Before you ran off, I was about to ask if you come here often. Then I realized that sounded like a bad pick-up line."

She laughs, and the sound is like bamboo wind chimes fluttering in the breeze. There's something about this woman that I like instantly. She's confident in herself, in a quiet, almost authoritative way; she's enjoying the outdoors; and she's cute. We walk on in companionable silence. When a snake suddenly slithers in front of me, I jump and she laughs, assuring me it's just a corn snake, nothing to be concerned about.

"You're not from here?" she asks.

"Philadelphia. I'm just traveling through."

A look of disappointment washes across her face before she quickly replaces it with her bright smile.

"Where are you headed?"

"Well...nowhere really." What I want to say is that before today I had no idea where I was headed, but that right now, I'll be headed to her front door, wherever it is, if she'll have me.

I watch as two squirrels dart in and out of the tree by our side, chasing each other round and round the trunk of the massive live oak.

"You live locally?" I make it sound as casual as I can.

"About an hour away. Gulfport. You've heard of it?"

I shake my head.

"It's just south of St. Petersburg."

"Is that the place someone told me about, where all the lesbians live?"

"Yep. One quarter of our 12,000 residents identify as LGBTQ."

"Maybe I should check it out." Another damn butterfly flutters through my stomach.

"Maybe you should."

We're back by the river where fast-flowing water rushes across dark boulders of solid limestone.

"I'm hooked up over there." I point across to the campground. "You want to see it?"

"Actually, I'm camping there too," she says, and we walk back together.

She stops in front of a very compact, one-person tent. "It was nice meeting you." She smiles and a dimple appears on one side of her face. "I hope you figure out where you're going."

"You too," I grin. "I mean, it was nice meeting you too. Doesn't look like you need help figuring out where you're going—you look as if you know already." I haven't sounded this ridiculous since I met Lizzie. Babbling like the river we just crossed.

I give a little wave and walk down to my campsite. Inside Uhura, I pull off my wet sneakers and put my Tevas on. Then I pull out my gravity chair and take it outside, along with my laptop.

I lower myself into my chair and pull up an article that needs a final edit. It's about Napoleon's second wife, Marie Louise, and although it's well written, I can't seem to focus on it. My mind keeps wandering over to the tent down the path where a cute dyke is probably calling her girlfriend to tell her about the dork she met on the trail today. What must I have looked like to her? My once-cropped hair has grown so long my bangs fall across my forehead and I have to push them to the side. I guess that could be considered attractive, in a lazy kind of way. I've put on weight, which is a good thing as my shirt and shorts fit better than they would have months ago. I'm a lot taller than her; always a positive in my mind, and maybe hers too.

I try to refocus my gaze on the page, to the birth of the future Napoleonic heir, but instead I find myself staring out beyond the trees to the river. Does she have a girlfriend?

I put the laptop back in Uhura and meander down the path.

She's sprawled in a low beach chair by her tent under the shade of an oak tree, her legs splayed out in front of her, her arms above her head. She might be asleep or meditating.

"Mind if I interrupt?"

She jumps, startled, then looks up and rewards me with a grin.

"I thought perhaps we could eat dinner together," I say. "I'm a lousy cook, but I have a delicious bottle of nonalcoholic sangria that might make up for my lack of ability in the kitchen."

She smiles, and my stomach turns a little somersault.

"You're in luck. I'm an excellent cook. If you have the ingredients, I'll turn it into a feast. Looks like we have everything we need for a very good evening together."

A shudder goes through me. Is it my excitement, or did Lizzie just walk on my grave?

Chapter Twenty-Six

The air is still hot and humid when Kat ambles over to my site a little later.

"Kat, meet Uhura," I say and she looks around, confused.

"My vehicle," I explain with a grin. "Uhura—from *Star Trek*?"

"You're a trekkie?"

"Nah. I never even watched it once. But I decided early on I wanted to give my motorhome a nickname. It's a Roadtrek, which sounded like Star Trek to me. I looked up the names of the women characters and discovered there was only one female in the original series."

I've set out two lawn chairs and a small table for us, and I pour two large glasses of sangria.

"There's no alcohol in it, so don't worry, I'm not trying to get you drunk."

She raises her eyebrows and says, "Cheers," as we clink glasses. Her green eyes smile at me and I feel them penetrate whatever armor I've been wearing lately.

"Here's looking at you kid," I respond and she smiles.

As I take a sip of my drink, a flash of lightning lights up the darkening sky. A moment later an enormous clap of thunder roars through the air.

"It's close," she says. "We better go inside."

"It's not raining. I love watching storms."

"Me too, but it's not safe. Tampa Bay is the lightning capital of the world. We locals know better than to stay outdoors when a storm starts. Too many people have been killed here."

Seems a little dramatic, but I pick up the sangria bottle and the little table it was on. We barely make it inside when the rain starts bucketing down.

"Hope your tent's waterproof," I say, hastily rearranging the interior so that we now have a table with seats on either side of it. Actually, I hope it's not. That way she may have to spend the night here.

"Yep. I camp plenty."

She looks around, admiring how carefully the rig was built so that every inch has a purpose. Her gaze alights on the small pewter urn that has Lizzie's ashes in it. I keep it by the bed, though I meant to move it.

"Here, let me show you what ingredients I have," I say, to distract her. "If you can make them into a feast, I'll be truly impressed."

We both get up at the same time. As she brushes past me, I spin her around and say, "I'm really glad you're here." I put a hand on the small of her back and pull her toward me. "I've wanted to do this ever since that first moment I saw you stalking that deer." I trail my other hand softly on her cheek as I lean in and kiss her. Her mouth is warm like a chocolate brownie right out of the oven, and her tongue tastes of sangria. I slip my hand under her tank top, but she moves it away and steps back.

"I have a meal to prepare," she says with a smile, and before I know it she's chopping vegetables in a frenzy.

She's right about being a good cook. It's just spaghetti and pasta sauce, but it's the best damn meal I've had in months.

"Where'd you learn to cook like that?"

Her dimple shows. "Culinary school."

"That explains it." I fork a piece of squash and pop it in my mouth.

"How about you?" she asks. "What do you do?"

I tell her I'm an editor for several journals and magazines, which is why I can work and travel at the same time. She tells me she's the assistant chef at a hotel, but that she's thinking of leaving to start her own business.

"That's all the boring stuff out the way," she says. "Now tell me who you really are."

I'm the woman who killed her wife because I was more devoted to her than she was to me.

"Nothing much to tell," I say.

"Come on." She tilts her head. "We all have deep, dark secrets."

"Tell me yours, then."

"Hmm..." Her mouth twitches. "My last girlfriend was so annoying, I cut her up in pieces and fed her to the alligators."

I know she's joking, but I can't laugh. I pick up my fork and twirl spaghetti around it. "Is your mom a good cook too?" I don't really like talking about families, but I need to head the conversation in a different direction, and this is the best I can think of.

"Are you kidding? One of the reasons she loves living in the U.S. is that she can take home doggy bags from restaurants or buy her food prepackaged and already prepared."

"She's not from here originally?"

"No. I was born in Israel. We moved here when I was a child, after my father was killed."

"Oh." I've always wondered how people can tell you their whole life story within minutes of meeting. I remember when I met Lizzie and on our very first date she mentioned that her parents had been killed in a car crash. She was waiting for me to say something about my own parents, but I wasn't about to tell her about a dad I never knew and a mom who abandoned me. People mouth platitudes when you tell them, but inside they're probably thinking, *what a loser.*

"He worked for a prominent Israeli company and was sent to Istanbul to negotiate an important contract. He never came back. They were ambushed by terrorists."

Aren't there any people with normal families? How come I seem to attract wounded puppies? Although I have to admit, Kat doesn't act as if she's wounded or like a puppy.

"Do you remember it? How old were you?"

"I was eight. Everyone tried to shield us from the news. Ima—my mom—told me he'd been in a car accident. But you can't keep that kind of thing from a child for long, especially not when it's splashed all over the news headlines. It was a big deal; the prime minister came to his funeral."

"Were you angry? Did you grow up hating the terrorists

and wanting revenge?"

Kat shakes her head. "No. You can't live your life that way. Everyone in Israel knows someone who died in a war or an attack. You move on. You have to."

Maybe it's because she was only eight that she's so naïve and so forgiving. It doesn't sound like her mom was though.

"But your mom left Israel. So she must have been angry."

"She got a really good job offer in the states. We were only going to stay for a year. But then my brother and I got settled in our schools, she started to enjoy the laid-back way of life, and somehow we ended up staying here."

"Have you been back?"

"Oh yes. Many times. I love to travel. I like seeing different cultures and learning about how they live. And of course, I collect recipes along the way."

Just like Ashley. She was always sending us postcards from some exotic place or other. Lizzie would smile indulgently—she preferred armchair travel with a good book—but I always thought Ash was running away from something. Why didn't she ever settle down and marry if she was such a good Christian woman? Isn't that what they're supposed to do?

"This was delicious." I place my napkin on the table. "Now it's time for dessert." I lean across the narrow table and pull her face toward me. We kiss and this time her mouth tastes like Italy.

I pull her up so we're standing opposite each other. I place both hands on her butt, pulling her tight into me. We kiss again, and my body starts to respond. I try to lift her tank top, but she pulls away.

"Uh-uh." She goes back to her seat, squeezed in at the table.

"Why not?"

"I don't know you."

"You've just spent the whole afternoon and evening with me. Of course you do."

"But you haven't told me anything about you. I can't make love with a stranger."

Who said anything about making love? I want to say. *It's just sex.*

"You know plenty about me. I'm an editor. I work from my RV. I've been on the road for a couple of months. And I like a beautiful redheaded woman." I slide in next to her and tousle her hair. "Though I have to say I didn't know people from the Middle East could be redheads."

Kat sighs. "Don't change the subject. You haven't told me anything about you really. For all I know you're an ax-murderer wanted by the police."

"If I were, I'd hardly tell you, would I?"

"You know what I mean."

"Anyway, I'd never use an ax. Far too messy." I feel my stomach tighten. *Oh Lizzie.* "Forget it," I say, standing up and moving as far away as I can in this tiny rig.

"Hey," she says softly. "I like you, okay? It's just that I don't jump into bed with women on a first date. Don't give up on me. Get to know me." She holds my hand and pulls me toward the sofa where we can sit next to each other.

"Tell me about your family. Or an ex-girlfriend. Or what you do when you're not editing."

"I love doing crosswords. The harder the better. It was something I had in common with—it's something I've always loved to do." Kat opens her mouth to interrupt, but I plow on quickly. "It helps keep my mind active. I like doing the cryptoquote and all the word puzzles in the newspaper. I like being challenged."

"I bet you like doing jigsaw puzzles too."

"No way. I don't have the patience for them. Fiddling about with all those little pieces." Kat looks disappointed. "I guess you enjoy them?"

"I do. It's so exciting to see a picture come together. I love how you can take individual pieces that are just blobs of things, and when you put them with other pieces, they make a coherent whole. It's like solving a difficult mystery. Perhaps that's what you are—a difficult mystery that needs solving. And maybe"—she pauses and her gaze penetrates right through me—"just maybe, I'll solve the mystery of you."

I don't know whether to be excited or appalled.

Chapter Twenty-Seven

Before Kat leaves, we make a plan to meet the next day and go dolphin spotting.

The drive from the park across Tampa and over a bridge spanning a sparkling bay is beautiful, but it's a long way from my campground. If I'm going to keep seeing Kat, I'll need to find somewhere closer. The marina sits on a causeway over the Intracoastal Waterway, halfway between the mainland and a barrier island. Kat's already sitting on a bench waiting for me. She looks adorable in tight, denim cut-offs and a tank top that tells the world how proud she is to be gay. We board a bright-yellow vessel, and within twenty minutes of sailing, several dolphins swim up and start frolicking in the wake of the boat. It's like a show you'd see at SeaWorld but better. A pair of dolphins arch and curve as they leap, their baby jumping next to them. Kat squeals in delight each time they leap out of the water. Afterward, we go downtown to St. Pete, where we buy gourmet ice pops in weird flavors like avocado and persimmon, and we lick each other's tongues, gleefully enjoying the crazy mix of tastes.

When I suggest we go back to her place she demurs. "Next time."

I like Kat, but I can't quite make her out. Is she stringing me along? I like that she's not as vapid as Bronzie was, but that doesn't mean I want to get +emotionally invested in her.

She's busy at work for the next few days, so I don't get to see her again until Monday, her day off.

We meet in her little town of Gulfport, the place that's purportedly so full of lesbians. Because it's the 3rd of July, flags are flying everywhere. Kat shows me the waterfront casino, which is used for dancing instead of gambling, and a parade of stores with funky window displays: a leather man draped in a fisherman's net, a manatee made out of bottle caps, lava lamps and shell jewelry. It takes a while to walk up the street because she seems to know everyone and they all stop to say hi.

"This is the Garrett, where I work." She indicates a hotel with Victorian spires and turrets that ought to look out of place among the brightly painted beachy bungalows. Somehow, it fits right in with all the other quirky buildings.

"And your house...?"

"Next time," she teases. "I promise."

We walk a few blocks and sit on a bench in a small park opposite the water. I move closer to her and kiss her. We make out ferociously, like teenagers in a darkened cinema.

When we take a break she says, "Come tomorrow for our 4th of July fireworks display. It's amazing."

I shake my head. "I don't think so."

I never manage to watch a firework display without remembering a little girl being set down by her mom in a crowded field and told not to move until she returned. How she watched the fireworks with amazement, but how after they'd finished, her mom still didn't come back.

"Oh, you must. We're a small town but the display is outsize. You don't want to miss it. Shore Boulevard is closed and we all bring our beach chairs and sit in the road right opposite the water where they set them off. I guarantee you'll have the best view you've ever had."

I used to think that maybe once I was an adult I could hold onto the feeling of wonder I had that evening, oohing and ahhing with everyone else as thousands of red, white and blue lights formed dazzling patterns in the sky then showered sparkles over the landscape. But that feeling was always accompanied by another one: abandonment.

"Brings back bad memories," I say, hoping she'll let it go.

"Then let's replace them with some good ones."

Kat's so different from Lizzie. Lizzie respected my reticence and didn't push me. For years, every July 4th, she went to a friend's place near the Art Museum and watched the city firework display from their balcony while I stayed home. She never wanted to pry into my history, so I never did tell her the full story of what happened with Mom. Maybe if I had, she'd have understood why her betrayal ruined everything.

"Come on," Kat says, "try it. And we'll come back to my place afterward. I promise."

Now *that's* an offer I can't refuse.

&

By the time we make our way down Beach Boulevard the next day, folks are streaming down the street from every direction, carrying their beach chairs and coolers. Young   couples with nose rings and tattoos push toddlers in strollers, long-haired gay men carry shih-tzus under their arms, while silver-haired lesbians push their lovers in wheelchairs. Kat spots friends who wave us over to sit with them.

A band is playing a tango and people of all ages kick up their knees, point their toes, and dip backwards, oblivious to how they look. There's an atmosphere of wild abandon and freedom.

The band falls silent and suddenly I hear a boom. The first fireworks hiss and explode in the air, dropping tears of blue and silver. Knots start to tie themselves in my stomach.

"I don't think I can do this," I mutter to Kat, but there's too much noise and she can't hear me.

More fireworks explode, filling the night with patriotic colors. Kat's friends clap delightedly.

You're an adult. This isn't Pennsylvania.

Kat glances over at me then touches my arm. "What's the matter?" She puts her mouth to my ear, so I can hear her. "You're shaking."

"Tell you later."

Music plays, fireworks dazzle, and I tell myself that I can handle it. Maybe even enjoy it. But my chest is thumping with the memory of how my heart cracked and splintered that day. I forced it shut and kept it that way until Lizzie came along.

I make it to the finale then tell Kat I need to leave.

"I'll come with you." She picks up the beach chairs and flings them over her shoulder.

Once we get away from the main drag, the streets are silent.

"Tell me," she says.

Will I tell her how everyone left and I remained in the field, hopping from one foot to the other, determined to wait for Mom?

It was dark and there was a chill in the air and I was terrified, but I stayed in the pasture, cold and scared, and kept myself awake by walking round and round in circles. Finally, just as light was breaking and the crows were starting to caw, Mom came staggering across the field, her whole body thick with the smell of alcohol.

"JP?"

It's not Mom, it's Kat's voice, pulling me back to the present.

"What happened?"

"The first time I ever saw a fireworks display, my mom got drunk and forgot about me for hours," I say tersely.

"Oh, you poor thing." Kat takes my hand in hers as we walk. "What did she say when she remembered you?"

"She apologized. Said it would never happen again."

The air is warm and street lamps outline the shapes of palm trees as geckos run across the sidewalk. I feel a million miles away from upstate Pennsylvania.

"My mom can be pretty forgetful too," Kat says, missing the point, missing it completely. "Was she a good mom, apart from that?"

"She wasn't the best mom, but she wasn't the worst either. She kept a roof over my head and food in my belly. Until she left again."

"Again?"

"She got involved with a man called Ed." I replay it all in my head, while Kat walks by my side.

He was tall and reasonably good-looking, but his eyes were yellow and he smelled of stale beer. She swore he only drank a can or two a day and that she wouldn't touch it.

He got a job interview in a town two hundred miles away. Mom was like a giddy little girl. I was more grown up than she was. You could see this loser wasn't going to get the kind of job they were talking about: floor supervisor at a large warehouse. He'd be lucky if they let him work on the factory line.

They left in the morning, and she assured me she'd be home that evening. I went to school, came home, did my homework, then sat by the window, watching for Ed's rusty pickup to come shuddering to a halt outside. It got dark so I heated up my dinner. I waited for a phone call, but none came. It was bedtime. I decided to stay up. I sat on the sofa watching TV until at some point I fell asleep. When I woke up, light was streaming in through the windows. I skipped school so I'd be home when they arrived, but the day passed and they didn't show. I started to get worried. I called all the hospitals in the area, but there were no reports of a woman with my mom's description, no records of her name.

Kat's waiting for me to say something. "She left with Ed to go on a job interview in the next state. Said if he got it we'd all move there."

"And did you?"

"No, because she didn't come back."

"Ever?" Even in the dark, I can see the look of horror on Kat's face.

"I didn't tell anyone Mom was missing because I knew what it would mean. I lied about my age and got a part-time job at a supermarket. I took care of the rent and paid the bills."

"How old were you? How long did it go on for?"

"I was sixteen. That was it. Never saw her again."

Although of course, that's not the entire truth. I won't tell Kat about the phone call that came four months later. How my heart flipped when I heard Mom's voice, and how much I wanted to feel her arms around me. I wanted it so badly I could almost smell the familiar scent of her cheap perfume filling the air. But when she said she was coming back I told her not to bother. I told her if she did, I'd call the police and tell social services that she'd been gone all that time, and she'd be arrested. Even though she was a lousy mom, I longed for her to be home. But there are some things you don't forget and you don't forgive. There are times you have to listen to your head and be strong, not give in to the foolish whims of a broken heart.

Back at Kat's apartment, she puts the beach chairs away and pours us both a soda.

We sit on the futon in her living room and she snuggles up to me.

"You're quiet," I say. "What happened to chatty Katty?"

"I'm still thinking about what you told me. I have such a close relationship with my mom, I can't imagine what you went through. Didn't you try to track her down once you were an adult?"

"Why would I do that?"

"To give her a piece of your mind, and tell her what an awful thing she did."

I laugh wryly. "You're so naïve. You don't think a mom who abandons her child knows that? It was the drink made her do it."

"You must have been so mad. Do you have a ton of anger inside you?"

She looks up at me, her eyes searching my face. Is she worried that I'm going to suddenly explode on her? She needn't be. Lizzie taught me how to control my anger. How to uncurl clenched fists and take deep breaths. She didn't teach me how to get even though. I figured that out for myself.

"Sure, I was mad at first, but I moved on."

"And you never wanted to find out if she got sober?"

"No. Because I wouldn't have let her back in my life anyway."

"I wish you could have fixed things with her somehow."

"Yeah, well..." I think of Lizzie. How I grew up telling myself I would never let myself fall in love. How Lizzie won me over, slowly, like a waterfall wearing away a rock. How I finally allowed myself to love again. And how it all came crashing down that morning. The morning after she abandoned me all night and then came home saying all the same things Mom said: *I'm sorry. I won't drink again.*

"Some things can't be fixed." My voice is gruff because I'm fighting back tears.

Kat hears the catch in my voice and probably thinks I'm referring to Mom.

"Perhaps one day you'll meet my mom. She's lovely. You'll like her. She has a super big heart. Spends her time rescuing stray cats and abandoned puppies."

I'm not interested in her mom. "But meanwhile," Kat says and inches closer to me on the sofa, "let's forget the past and the future, and focus on the present."

She unbuttons my shirt and pulls my breasts free from captivity. Her hands start kneading them and I feel my body respond. I moan as every part of me starts to tingle. She leans forward and starts licking me, and it feels so good I'm ready to explode. Her fingers dance over my body and I thrust myself toward her, moving her hand down to my crotch.

"Not yet," she whispers, continuing to touch and lick my breasts. I pull on the waistband of her shorts and thrust my hand inside.

"No!" She jerks away.

"Then go down on me," I command, but instead she lifts her head and looks at me, frowning.

"I don't want to have sex, I want to make love. Long languorous love. We have the whole night, and I want to make it special."

I don't want it to be special. Lizzie was special. She was the one I loved, the one who made love to me. I just want to screw.

"Come on," I say gruffly, "don't be a cunt-tease."

Kat sits up abruptly. "Is that what you think? Is that all I am to you? I thought when you confided in me, it meant something. Was it just to get inside my pants?"

"What about you?" I say. "Do you get off on other people's misery? If I'd given you an even bigger sob story would you have had an orgasm without me even touching you?"

I pull away from her and button up my shirt with shaking fingers.

We stare at each other. I know what will happen next and I wait, patiently.

Finally, she says it. "I'm sorry."

I put my arm around her. "It's okay," I say.

And so it begins. The dance of love. Except, of course, that I will never love her. At least, not like I loved Lizzie.

I was devoted to Lizzie.

PART THREE

ASHLEY

Chapter Twenty-Eight

"Here's what we know so far. She sold the house and her truck. But we don't know anything else. She could be anywhere at all."

It's reassuring to have Paula and Cleo's faces opposite me on the screen as we Skype together. It took a few days and a little detective work by all of us for the truth to sink in: JP had disappeared on purpose.

"I still don't understand why she did it. I tried so hard to be a good friend to her," Paula says. "Obviously, I wasn't good enough. I hate to think of her all alone in the world, with no support system."

"You did your best. She's a tough nut," Cleo says. "She always keeps everything close to her chest."

"Are you worried about her?" I ask, somewhat disingenuously.

"Of course," they both say at once.

"Then maybe we should try to find her."

"I don't think she wants to be found," Cleo says. "If she wanted to be in contact, she'd have given us forwarding information and kept her cell phone and email active."

"Not necessarily," Paula says, and I could fall on my knees and thank her. I need them to want to find JP as much as I do, even if it's for entirely different reasons. "People do crazy things when they're in their first year of grieving. That's why counselors tell people not to make any changes. It's a natural tendency to do something drastic like JP has. I'm super worried that she could eventually try and harm herself if she doesn't have any of us around to give her support."

"Are you worried about that too?" Cleo turns her attention to me, and even though there's a screen between us, I feel my heart thump and my stomach tighten. I want to be able to interact with Cleo as a friend, as I do with Paula, but every time those dark eyes turn toward me, I feel as if I'm melting. I tear my attention back to the left-hand side of the screen, to Paula's plump, friendly face and concerned   expression.

"I don't know what to think." I've toyed with the idea of telling them both my suspicions, but I don't want them to think I'm crazy or that I'm displacing my grief. Paula seems to know plenty about the grieving process, and I can imagine her agreeing with Dr. Lim's assessment and telling me I need to focus on my own feelings instead of some off-the-wall theory about Lizzie's death. If we're going to find JP, I need them to think it's because we all share the same concern, not because I believe she might have harmed my sister.

In my head, I always use that word, harm. Even when I'm thinking, I can't bring myself to say that JP may have killed my sister. It sounds too insane.

I look up and see Paula waving at me from the screen. "Earth to Ashley. Are you still with us?"

"Sorry. Just trying to figure out where she might be."

"She could have taken a plane to just about anywhere," Cleo says.

"I don't think she'd have done that," Paula says. "Even if she got rid of everything from the house, nobody could fit all their belongings into two suitcases. Wherever she's gone, I'll bet she used a vehicle to get there."

"Then why sell the truck? She could have bought a cover for the cab of the pickup which would have given her a ton of storage room."

"I know why," I say. "When I visited her she was all excited about the possibility of buying an RV. I bet she replaced the truck with a vehicle that gave her living space as well as storage."

Paula nods her head vigorously. "Yes. I remember she mentioned something about a motorhome to me too."

"Cleo, you're the one who found out about the house and truck. Can you find out what she might have bought, so we can try to track her down?" I ask.

Cleo shakes her head. "Searching public records for home and vehicle ownership is easy. But you can't go backwards. You can't put in someone's name and find out what they own."

"Then how on earth could we find her?" I feel frustrated but hopeful that three heads will be better than one.

"Did she ever mention family anywhere? Where's she from originally?" Cleo asks.

"Upstate Pennsylvania. But I don't think she'd ever go back there."

"She used to complain about how cold Philly was. Maybe she decided to go to California," Paula says.

"Florida would be closer," I say. *And California might bring her too close to me.*

"Yeah, but she was always pretty dismissive of Florida. New York with palm trees she used to call it."

After the rapid-fire back-and-forth, there's a lull in the conversation.

"She could be traveling around without any destination in mind at all. Lots of women do that. There's even a whole group for them," Paula says.

"It's like finding a needle in a haystack," I say despondently.

"Hold on a minute." Cleo has perked up suddenly. "What do you mean a whole group?"

"RV women, camping women, traveling women..."

"How do they organize themselves? Do they have set places they rendezvous?"

"I'm not sure. There may be a couple of formal organizations, and some of it may just be Facebook groups. I can ask Doris. She's done it."

"I don't see how that will help us." I want to remain optimistic, but it's hard.

"Don't you see? Even though JP's not on Facebook, most people are. If we join those groups, we can put the word out that we're looking for her. If she really did purchase an RV, eventually we'll locate her."

After I get off the phone I mull over what I'll do if we do find her. Now that I have no job, I could go to wherever she is. I have some savings I can use. But how would I approach her? What would I say?

Hi, JP, nice to see you again. Did you kill my sister?

Chapter Twenty-Nine

Three days later Cleo messages me to ask if we can Skype. A moment later, her face fills my screen.

"I've found her!"

"How?"

"Just like we said: I reached out to a bunch of Facebook groups. Said I wanted to surprise my dear friend JP by showing up with a gift for her, but that I lost all my contacts when I dropped my phone over the side of my fishing boat."

"Fishing boat? Cleo, I didn't know you could be so deceptive."

"Figured I needed an excuse that would work for those outdoors types." She smiles. Her dark eyes are so warm and inviting I feel as if I want to reach out through the laptop and hug her.

"Where is she?"

"Florida."

"Are we sure it's her?"

"The woman who answered my post, Gail, said she and her friends had hung out with JP at a state park in Georgia a week ago. They invited her to join them in Florida, and she assured them she'd be there."

Now that Cleo's found JP, I'm not sure what I want to do. Jump on a plane and confront her? And if so, with what? I don't have all the answers. In fact, I hardly have any of them. The only thing I'm pretty sure about is that Lizzie was trying to tell me it was JP who poisoned her. I'm not too certain about anything else. Did she do it over the course of years like the Munchausen by proxy woman who killed her kid? Did she cause Lizzie's health to deteriorate to such a fragile state that if Lizzie got drunk it would kill her? How did she get Lizzie to agree to drink alcohol? Helen said they were going out to celebrate, but JP doesn't drink and Lizzie spent years celebrating without drinking, so why would she have imbibed so much alcohol that she walked into the E.R. reeling?

"... Ashley?" I jump, startled. Cleo has evidently been trying to say something but couldn't get my attention.

"Huh?"

"I was telling you more about the camping women, but you were miles away. What's going on?"

She leans in toward the screen but I glance away. It's too hard to ignore the increase in my heartbeat those penetrating eyes cause. She misconstrues my avoidance.

"Is there some reason you want to find JP that you haven't told me?"

Should I tell her? I'd like to share the burden of my suspicions with someone, but she might think I'm crazy and I don't want her to think badly of me.

"No, I...was just thinking."

"What will you do now that we've located her? I was going to tell Gail to say something to her, then I thought I better wait."

"I'm glad you did," I say quickly. She cocks her head to one side like an inquisitive puppy.

"Why is it so important that she not know we're looking for her?"

I remind Cleo that we have no idea what her state of mind is and we don't want to upset her. She nods then says something I didn't expect.

"I have a few days' vacation coming up. Why don't you and I meet her there?"

This time I feel more than just an increased heartbeat. My whole stomach seizes up. But in a good way. The kind of way I used to feel on Christmas Eve, after we came home from midnight mass and put out the milk and cookies for Santa. I try to think of an excuse for why this is not a good plan. Nothing comes to mind.

We agree to research airfares and to talk tomorrow.

Two days later I step out of the terminal into the

suffocating summer air of Jacksonville and the warm embrace of Cleo. I've told myself that spending time with Cleo is a terrible idea, but it will be much better to face JP with someone at my side. I have no idea what I'm going to say, or how she may react, so a buffer person may be very important.

Cleo's already picked up the rental car and has directions to the southern part of Amelia Island where the state park is. The terrain getting there is like nothing I've ever seen before: miles and miles of flat green lowlands punctuated with narrow waterways. I'm struck by the contrast with my familiar Sierra foothills. How do people get any exercise when there's nothing to climb?

Cleo hasn't told Gail that we're coming. If JP's there, we don't want anyone to spill the beans.

"Do you think she'll be pleased to see us?" Cleo asks.

"Hard to say."

"I know, right? It's so hard to know why she just upped and left without telling any of us."

I used to think that, but I don't anymore. I'm pretty sure JP is carrying around a very guilty secret, even though I haven't yet figured out exactly what it is. Her reaction to seeing us may tell me all I need to know.

We tell the park ranger that we're here to see friends, and we give him Gail's name. He directs us to the campground across the road. We pass some smaller sites and find her site number. It's a small area facing a creek. An enormous trailer sits on the site, and another one opposite it, though the vehicles that would pull them are nowhere in sight. Camping chairs are set up in a circle around a table with several empty beer buckets on it, but the place is deserted.

"You said Gail told you JP has a Roadtrek. Let's drive around and look for it," I say, having thoroughly researched exactly what the camper looks like.

A quick circuit of the small campground yields nothing.

"Don't be discouraged," Cleo says. "She's probably driven somewhere with Gail and her friends. They'll be back before too long,"

I nod, wondering what to do until then.

"Let's go across the road and walk down to the beach," Cleo says. "I bet it's beautiful."

It's so hot and I'm so sweaty, it's the last thing I want to do, but there's nothing else around, so I agree to it.

We use the bathrooms to change, and it's a relief to get out of my T-shirt and capris and feel the air tickle my back as I put on my skimpiest tank top and lightest cotton shorts. Cleo's done before I am, and when I come out and see her bending over the trunk to put her suitcase back into it, a smile comes unbidden to my face. In shorts, her long, dark legs are spectacular. There's no other word for it. I want to run up to her and grab her from behind, feel that beautiful black butt nestled in my pelvis.

The moment the thought comes into my mind, I'm horrified. I'm here to find out the truth about Lizzie's death, but instead I'm admiring the rear end of a gorgeous woman. What is wrong with me?

I fling my case onto the backseat of the car and take off quickly toward the beach.

"Wait for me," Cleo calls out. I start running down the long wooden boardwalk. I pick up my pace barely registering the flower-covered sand dunes that rise up toward me. I run past them and onto a white-sand beach that stretches for miles. Without turning back to see where Cleo is or what she's doing, I head to the ocean and start sprinting parallel to it.

I'm furious at myself. I should never have allowed Cleo to come with me. I should have come by myself, or asked Paula if she'd accompany me. I knew what was going on between me and Cleo, I knew it! Who was I kidding when I kept asking myself so naïvely why my heart raced and thumped every time I saw her? Or why my palms were sweaty and my stomach tight when she touched my shoulder or showed any sign of support?

I succumbed to those urges once, and I've spent years assuring myself that I never will again. I may not be married to Jesus like the Catholic nuns are, but I will not be disloyal to him. I will not be like my sister.

My feet pound the sand and I pick up speed, determined to outrun my feelings.

"Don't overdo it!" a guy sitting on a beach chair yells as I run past him.

What does he know? I speed up even though I have no water with me. The punishing sun beats down on me, and

I'm glad. Maybe it will beat some sense into me. A hot ocean breeze brushes my face and the sweat pours down my back. I'm drenched, but it feels good to do something healthy with my body. Maybe the run will purify me of the toxins that feel like they're filling my body. I can hear Lizzie's voice in my head, "It's not a sin, Ash, not when you love someone. Not if it's your nature." But I won't listen. I won't. Lizzie gave in to her desires and look how she ended up.

I brush the sweat out of my eyes and keep running.

Chapter Thirty

Someone is splashing water on my face and I sit up and cough.

"What the—!"

I splutter as a man who looks vaguely familiar says, "You collapsed. Looks like you fainted. I don't know where you're from, but you can't run like that in the Florida afternoon sun."

People start to gather around me.

"Are you okay?" An elderly woman in a floppy sun hat bends down toward me. "Drink this." She offers a clear bottle with amber liquid in it. I look cautiously at it. "It won't poison you." She laughs. "It's just Gatorade." I gulp on the drink gratefully. My head is pounding, but I'm starting to come around.

"We don't have lifeguards on this beach. Should we call an ambulance?" The guy who splashed water on me looks concerned, but I assure him I'll be okay. He's wearing blue swim trunks and has an extremely tight six-pack. His hair is blond and he brushes it out of his face as he speaks.

"I'm sorry I was an idiot," I say, smiling up at him. "You warned me, but I didn't listen."

"No worries." He seems like a nice guy. Could I be attracted to him? My body hasn't sent me any signals yet, but after all, I just fainted. My electrolytes are off, so maybe my sensors are as well.

"What happened?" I look around and there's Cleo, her voice filled with concern. I look away quickly.

Cool guy fills her in.

"You okay to walk back?" she asks.

"Give me another couple of minutes." I don't want

to have to lean on her.

"I'm Kyle," my rescuer says. "Where are you two from?"

Cleo makes small talk with him, and I decide I'm ready to stand up. I put my hands on the ground by my side, ready to push up, but Kyle sees and immediately offers his hand. "Let me help you." He pulls me up in one swift movement.

"Thanks." I smile. "You've been great." I turn to Cleo. "I'm okay now. We can go."

We start walking down the beach and Kyle walks with us.

"I'm staying at a B&B in Fernandina Beach if you two want to visit while you're down," he says and tells us the name of it.

We thank him and leave him at his beach chair.

"What was that about?" Cleo asks.

"What?"

She does her best imitation of a valley girl. "You've been great," she mimics. "Can I get in your pants?"

I snort. "Are you jealous?"

The moment I say it, I realize it's completely the wrong thing to say.

"Should I be?" She grabs my hand and turns to face me. "Do we need to talk?"

I shake my head. "Let's get back to the campground. Maybe Gail and the others are back by now."

She drops my hand as if it were contaminated. "Fine," she mutters.

We walk in silence.

"Why did you run off like that? If you'd told me you wanted to go for a run, I'd have given you a bottle of water to take."

"Sorry," I say, then, realizing how much I need her to be on my side when we talk to JP, I turn and say, "Truly, Cleo, I'm sorry. I have a lot on my mind and thought a run might clear my head."

She smiles. "That's a relief. I thought I'd done something to upset you the way you took off like that."

When we get back to the campground, Gail's site is filled with women. Two enormous pickup trucks are parked alongside. I practically sprint over in my anxiety to find JP.

"Gail?" I ask the first woman in my path, a pretty blonde woman with enormous breasts.

"No, I'm Darlene."

"I'm Gail," the woman sitting opposite her says, looking puzzled. "And you are...?"

Cleo walks up behind me. "We're Facebook friends. I'm Cleo."

Gail looks confused, and then the realization dawns on her. "The one looking for JP?"

"Yes," I say, too anxious to exchange any more pleasantries. "Is she here?"

Gail shakes her head. "Uh-uh."

"No?" My whole being fills with disappointment. "Is she coming?"

"She said she would," the pretty blonde woman says. "She promised."

"Darlene and JP were quite the item up in Georgia. All over each other."

I feel myself recoil. That's why JP is coming? She's already chasing another woman? So soon after Lizzie? All that grief, all that crying and clawing, and two months later she's moved on?

Gail invites us to sit and offers us a cold beer. I accept mine gratefully and sink into an empty chair as far from Darlene as I can get. Cleo sits next to Gail and I can't help noticing Darlene's gaze sweeping up and down, checking her out. But if JP's her type, then I hardly think I have much to worry about. Damn. I have to stop thinking like that.

It starts to get dark and another woman in the group begins throwing logs into the fire ring.

"Does it get cold in the evening?" I ask, thinking of the Sierra Nevadas and how quickly the air cools down after the sun sets even on the hottest of days.

"Sure. If you consider 80 degrees cool." The woman laughs. "We just like to watch the flames and make s'mores."

"Where are y'all staying?" Gail asks. "Fernandina Beach?"

I shake my head. We didn't book anything because we had no idea what was going to happen with JP.

"We don't have a place yet," Cleo replies.

"Stay with us," Gail says. "Our motorhome is enormous. The second bedroom has a double bed so you'll be nice and cozy." She winks.

"We couldn't," I say with a gulp at the same time as Cleo says warmly, "That would be great. Thanks so much."

The rest of the evening passes in a blur of good food, bawdy jokes and too much beer. Even the stars seem to be laughing with us as they twinkle between the oak trees and pine scrub. At first all I can think about is how I'm going to handle this evening's sleeping arrangements, but Cleo barely looks at me. She seems more taken with a woman called Rosa who has skin as white as mine and hair as black as Cleo's, but straighter. They seem to be sharing a very animated conversation. Will Cleo be taking Gail up on her offer of sleeping accommodations or has she found a better one?

By midnight I'm completely exhausted. I left my house at five this morning and even though it's three hours   earlier in California, it's been a very long day.

"I'm heading inside," I tell Gail, and when I get up, it seems it's a signal for everyone else as well. I was hoping I could be in bed and asleep before Cleo came in.

Gail shows us where everything is, and after performing a very quick toilette, I jump into the double bed. I try desperately to fall asleep but I'm still wide awake when Cleo climbs into the bed several minutes later. I lie still with my eyes closed and sense her turn on her side to face me.

"Ashley?" she whispers. I say nothing. Maybe I can convince her I'm asleep. "Ash?"

All of a sudden I feel her lips brush mine. They're soft and warm and send waves of electricity pulsing through me. I open my mouth to say no, but she takes it as an invitation and clamps her lips on mine more firmly. Instinctively I pull her toward me. I want her badly. I want her with a desperation I haven't felt since college. Her kiss deepens and a flood of desire threatens to drown me. I pull my head back and push her away. Even as I do, I notice how the skin of her breastbone feels beneath my hand.

"No!" My whisper is loud and urgent.

"Why?" She takes my hand and places it gently above her breast.

"I can't. I'm a Christian."

"So am I. So are lots of lesbians."

I pull my hand away. "I'm not a lesbian. Why do you say that?"

"Forget the label," she says softly. "You're attracted to me, aren't you?"

I say nothing.

"I'm attracted to you too. And it's been a very long time since I felt this way. I lost my partner to cancer five years ago."

"I'm so sorry," I say.

"I haven't wanted anyone since then. Until you."

Five years and JP couldn't even wait five months.

"I wouldn't be your first, would I?" She props herself up on her elbow so she can look at me.

I can't speak. I don't want to answer.

"What happened? Something long ago?"

"In college," I whisper.

"What made you so scared?"

I turn to face her. "I'm not scared. I just don't want to live a life of sin. All I've ever wanted is a normal life—to get married, have kids, and be part of a tight-knit church community."

"You're thirty-five years old and you haven't done any of that. Perhaps there's a reason."

"I just haven't met the right—"

"Come on, Ash. Stop kidding yourself." She sounds frustrated and I feel her pull away. "You've met the right guy a hundred times. He's sitting in your church; singing in your choir; a widowed parent of one of your students. You meet him everywhere. But you're not interested in him. You don't notice him." An image comes to mind of Kyle today. How sweet and attentive he was. How much I wanted to be attracted to him.

I sigh. So does Cleo.

"I'm not going to push you. You're going to have to figure it out for yourself." She swings her legs over the side of the bed. "There's a sofa in the front part of the motor home. I'll sleep there."

As she walks out of the room, it's as if a heavy curtain is drawn across my heart. Every nerve in my body is on fire. But my head has a different message.

Look what happened the last time you gave in.

Chapter Thirty-One

"Lovers' tiff?" Gail says as I walk bleary-eyed and sleepless into the kitchen.

"Huh?"

"Cleo's already gone for a walk. I couldn't help noticing she slept on the sofa."

She thinks we're... "Cleo and I are just friends."

"Really?" She raises her eyebrows in surprise. "That's not what it looks like from where I stand."

I shake my head and pour myself a cup of coffee. "Let's talk about JP. Did she for sure say she was going to join you?"

"She promised Darlene she would. But if she's not here by now, I suspect she's not coming. It was probably JP's way of letting her down easy."

This morning is getting worse and worse.

"So our trip was wasted." It was crazy. Flying all the way out here from California, especially now that I have no job and have to be careful with money. I allowed myself to get so excited about finding JP and spending time with Cleo, that I wasn't thinking straight.

"Why do you want to find her so badly? Cleo said she had something for her, but there's something else isn't there?"

I'm beyond caring what this stranger thinks of me. "JP was married to my sister, Lizzie, who died two months ago. I think JP may have had a hand in it."

"You think JP killed her? How did your sister die?"

I tell her the whole story. Everything. Not leaving out a thing. She sits and listens, gulping coffee from a large travel mug, saying nothing.

"So you think JP was making her sick for years," she says

when I'm finished. "But why did she say, 'after the gym'? And what did she mean by 'in the water' and 'no energy'?"

"I don't know. I still think it must have something to do with the swimming pool. That she was saying she had no energy after her swim or maybe during it. What could JP have done to her in the pool?"

"The first thing I thought of was that JP put something in Lizzie's water, a drug or something, and that's why she had no energy. So by the time they left the gym, it was easy for JP to get her drunk."

"How did she know that getting her drunk would lead to her complete kidney failure? I've read stuff about FSGS, and some people can drink even with that condition."

"I don't know. You said she was in recovery. Could suddenly drinking a lot of alcohol induce some kind of alcohol poisoning?"

Alcohol poisoning. Is that what Lizzie meant?

"So you don't think I'm crazy? That I'm trying to find a reason for my sister's death because I'm grieving?"

Gail shakes her head. "You might be crazy—I don't know you well enough to judge." I'm taken aback but Gail is smiling and there's a twinkle in her eye. "And you're grieving that's for sure."

"You've met JP. Could you imagine her doing anything to a spouse she was devoted to?"

"I didn't get to know her well enough. Darlene might be the better person to talk to about that, although between you and me, she's not the sharpest pencil in the box. But I wouldn't rule anything out. I've worked with a lot of killers, and most of them looked as innocent as a baby in swaddling."

This time it's my turn to raise my eyebrows.

"I'm retired law enforcement," she says. "Went in when I was twenty, retired when I was forty."

I stand up to refill my coffee and while my back is still turned to Gail she asks, "What does Cleo make of all this?"

"I haven't told her." I turn around in time to see a look of extreme surprise register on Gail's face.

"You've told me and not her?"

"I don't want her to think badly of me. I—"

"But you're 'just friends.'" Gail draws air quotes and smiles knowingly. "Why does it matter so much what she thinks?"

I'm saved from answering when the woman in question walks through the door. She's wearing the same shorts she had on yesterday and a T-shirt that proclaims, 'Every Shade of Brown is Beautiful.' She's pulled her braids into a chignon and her arms and legs glisten with sweat. I drop my gaze.

"How was your walk?" Gail asks.

"Awe-inspiring. I was filled with gratitude for our amazing world."

It's how I feel when I'm surrounded by the glory of nature too.

"Gail doesn't think JP's going to come here," I say.

Cleo turns to Gail. "Do you have any idea where she might have gone instead?"

She shakes her head. "She didn't seem to have a plan."

Cleo heads for the shower and I decide I should take a run too.

I cross the road and head down the boardwalk to the beach. As I run, I try to piece everything together. Gail thinks Lizzie was saying she had no energy because JP had put something in her water. But Helen never mentioned seeing anything like that. She said Lizzie was excited about going out to dinner. So when did she lose her energy? Did JP give her something Lizzie thought would boost her energy but which actually was high-proof alcohol?

Nothing explains Lizzie's kidney failure. Sure her kidneys were already compromised by FSGS, and JP probably knew drinking alcohol wasn't a good idea for someone with that condition, but she couldn't have known it would lead to kidney failure. But what if she didn't want it to lead to kidney failure? *What if it was an accident?*

Despite the warm air, I feel a chill run through me because an idea is starting to form, and as I jog along the edge of the water, it's all starting to come together. Maybe JP was just trying to make Lizzie sick and never intended for her to die. This would tie in with Lizzie being hospitalized a month earlier. What if JP only meant for Lizzie to be hospitalized and then recover like she did the previous time? I'm reminded of the article about the woman who kept getting her kid hospitalized. What if JP had Munchausen by proxy and wanted to keep Lizzie sick, but instead something happened and Lizzie ended up dying? It would explain why JP was so distraught after Lizzie died. She was beside herself at the hospital, and in the garden when I saw her throwing dirt in her own face. Maybe she was furious not only at Lizzie, but at herself for messing it all up.

When Luke read me the article he said we should pray for that woman. I wondered how he could have so much compassion for someone who killed their child, but he reminded me that she was mentally ill. My sister is dead and if JP did it, whether on purpose or by accident, I can't feel sorry for her. But I can pray for her. I can pray that when I find her, she's willing to tell me the truth. And that she gets help and never does this to anyone else.

I stop running and slowly fall on my knees. *Heavenly Father...*

When I get back to the campground, Cleo tells me she has a plan for today.

"Let's drive up to the northern end of this barrier island. Gail says there's a town with cute shops and restaurants and a state park with a fort. She thinks JP might have gone to that state park instead of this one. If she's not there, we can just hang out—strictly as friends—and get to know each other."

"What about tonight? Will we stay up there or come back here?"

"I guess that depends if we find JP. But either way we can find a place to stay that has separate rooms. How would that be?"

I'm so relieved I could hug her. "Sounds perfect."

Amelia Island and Fernandina Beach are so pretty I could stay here forever. I've always loved the California coast with its dramatic cliffs and waves pounding the rocks. But here the wide, flat expanses provide a feeling of peace and tranquility. When we get to Fort Clinch State Park we drive directly to the campground. There are tents and RVs scattered throughout but no Roadtrek. Then we remember there's a second campground and drive over to that one. As we drive through, my chest seizes like a fist.

"There!" I point.

The site is set back from the road and the van is parked beneath the shade of a spreading oak. There's a single beach chair propped up against it. The wooden table on the site is bare.

My heart starts pounding so hard, I have to remind myself that I'm the one who always keeps her cool.

Cleo pulls the car to the side of the road.

"Let's go," she says, as I sit there almost paralyzed.

With hands like lead, I undo my seatbelt and step out of the car.

We walk into the site and Cleo goes up to the door.

"JP?" she calls out.

I hear a noise. Someone's in there. My heart thuds even harder.

"JP?"

We wait, but whoever is in there doesn't answer.

I go up to the door and rap on it with my knuckles. "Hello?" I knock again, as hard as I can. I hear shuffling and the door cracks open.

"Who's there?"

I can't see the person behind the door and the voice sounds muffled.

"We're looking for our friend," I say.

"Our *dear* friend," Cleo adds for emphasis.

The door slams shut. Is it her? Did she recognize us?

"Please," I call through the door. "We just want to make sure you're okay. We'll go away if you just come out."

The door opens a little more. A middle-aged woman in a dressing gown, her hair in curlers, and a cigarette in her mouth says, "I'm fine. Go away." She slams the door shut.

Cleo starts laughing. "Oh my goodness. Definitely not JP."

How can she laugh? I'm so disappointed. She puts her arm through mine. "Come on, think of the great story it'll make when we tell the girls at the campground. Especially that Darlene."

I chuckle. Yes, I can't see Darlene going after the woman in the dressing gown.

"Let's check in with the park ranger. Maybe he knows if JP was here."

We drive back to the entrance and Cleo uses all her charm to explain to the rangers how we're searching for our friend. They assure us they've been working all week and haven't seen anyone of JP's description. It's disappointing, but not entirely unexpected.

We decide to get something to eat before we head back. We choose a cafe on the main street that has delicious looking sandwiches and desserts on display under large glass pastry cases.

"Those croissants look heavenly," Cleo says.

"I wonder how many calories they have." I eye them longingly.

"If you want one, have one. The only problem for me is which one to choose: the amazing looking savory one, or the decadent hazelnut-chocolate?"

We agree to buy a spinach-avocado and a chocolate-berry and split them between us.

Once seated, I pick up my knife to cut them, but Cleo stops me. She pulls apart the savory croissant then leans forward and puts a piece in my mouth.

The flaky pastry, sweet spinach and mild avocado melt in my mouth, and when Cleo brushes the crumbs off my lip with her finger, something else melts too.

I cock my head to one side.

"Couldn't resist." She smiles and pops a piece of the pastry into her own mouth. I feel comfortable with Cleo, surprisingly so, since she's unlike anyone I know.

"Who's Audre Lorde?" I ask, reading off the side of the canvas bag hanging on her chair.

"Only one of the most amazing African American feminists to ever live. Have you not heard of her because she's a feminist or an African American?"

"Both probably. I've never been into feminism."

"Why? Don't you care about women's rights?"

"I do, but in my church a woman can get into trouble if she's too assertive."

I tell Cleo about the incident with Mike, and Pastor Timothy's reaction to it. When I finish, she looks appalled.

"You do know not all churches are like yours, don't you?" She tells me about the church she belongs to. "We're gay, straight, black, white. We thrive on diversity."

"I don't think we have any people of color at my church,"

I say. "I've never had an African American friend."
I hope I don't sound prejudiced, but Cleo leans
forward and takes my hand. "Well you do now." That
familiar tingle ripples through my body and makes me hot
all over.

&

We're drinking margaritas with Gail and her friends
at the campground when my cell phone rings. I don't
recognize the number, but it has a Philadelphia prefix so
I swipe it anxiously.
"Miss Glynn?" The voice is familiar though I can't
place it.
"Speaking." My voice is wary.
"This is Dr. Patel. We met last month at—"
"Yes! I know who you are." My heart starts racing.
Has he found something that will finally help me figure
out what happened to Lizzie?
"I don't know when you'll next be in Philadelphia, but
when you are, perhaps we could have a drink together."
The excitement drains out of me like water swirling
out of a filled bathtub. Really? He's coming on to me? I'm
ready to politely hang up, when he says in his singsong
voice, "I've been thinking more about your sister."
Now the bathtub of excitement is filled up again.
"Yes, yes, of course. I'm listening."
"It's not something I'm comfortable talking about on
the telephone. I'd rather we meet in person. Do you know
when you may be back east?"
"Actually, right now I'm in Florida so—"
"Oh, but that's perfect. I'm coming to Florida for a
conference this weekend. Why don't we meet at the
conference hotel?"
He tells me where he'll be. After we hang up, I grab
the bottle of margarita mix, excited.
"Who was that?" Cleo asks.
"Lizzie's doctor."
"Why would he be calling you?" She looks puzzled.
"I—I had some questions about Lizzie's condition.
How it might affect me. Genetics and stuff."
I try to sound vague and turn quickly to Gail.

"How far is Tampa from here?"

"Not that far. Three or four hours' drive," Gail says. "Why?"

"I think we're going to head over there in a couple of days."

"While you're in the Bay area, you should check out St. Pete and Gulfport. They're fun places and—oh!" She stops suddenly and we all look startled.

"I just remembered. We told JP about Gulfport. How gay-friendly it is. She seemed pretty interested. It's on the west coast of Florida and we're on the east. Amelia Island would have been the opposite direction for her from Amicalola. Maybe she skipped us and went there instead."

The news just keeps getting better and better. I'm so excited, I'm ready to leave this moment. Not only might Dr. Patel have some crucial information for me, but I may finally be on JP's track.

I know there's a possibility she won't be there. But what if she is?

Chapter Thirty-Two

Freeway traffic is so heavy that a four-hour drive turns into six. By the time we reach Gulfport, we're more than ready to stretch our legs. We dump our bags in the small hotel we found on the main drag and head out.

The main street, Beach Boulevard, is a quirky mix of arts and crafts galleries, upscale boutiques, and picturesque restaurants housed in stately Victorians or colorful mid-century bungalows. The street is wide and lined with trees that spread their leafy canopies to provide welcome shade from the heat. Spanish moss drapes itself over the limbs of spreading oaks.

"This is so quaint. I never knew Florida had small towns like this." I feel like a tourist as we walk past an eclectic-looking store with tie-dye shirts, mosaic lampstands, and rainbow mobiles hanging in the window.

"Me neither," Cleo says. "It feels tropical and exotic, and yet at the same time quintessential small-town USA. Except for the fact that I feel comfortable here."

"What do you mean?"

"As a woman of color. Small towns in the USA are nearly always either all white or all black. And have you noticed all the gay couples we've passed?"

I've seen several pairs of older women, but it hasn't occurred to me they were gay. How does she know? Maybe they're just retirees spending time together.

We walk the length of the street down to the water, where there's a stunning view of the bay that leads out to the Gulf of Mexico. As we walk out onto the pier, a movement catches my eye—the arch of a dolphin's back. We watch as two dolphins jump and frolic in the waves, before disappearing beneath the water.

Devoted

We turn around and head for a place to eat.

"This place is small," Cleo says as we cross the road and head back. "If JP's here, we'll run into her."

I've been thinking the same thing.

We decide to eat at the hotel and flop wearily into wicker armchairs on the outdoor patio. It's still hot and a wind has kicked up, which makes it feel tropical.

"I've never had fried green tomatoes," I tell the waitress, a young Asian woman with short hair and dimples, when she asks if we want appetizers.

"And cornbread with jalapenos? Count me in," Cleo tells her.

They are so delicious, Cleo asks if she can compliment the chef. I've never done anything like that, but Cleo assures me she does it all the time. "Don't you think they want to know when customers enjoy their food?"

"I guess so. I've just never thought of doing it."

A petite woman about our age approaches our table.

"Hi." She leans forward to shake our hands. "I'm Kat." She's wearing an enormous white apron and stray strands of red hair peek out from her chef's cap. "You asked to see me?" She looks apprehensive.

"These appetizers were wonderful," Cleo says. Immediately the chef's shoulders slump in relief. I guess most people only call her out when there's a problem.

"In that case, after you've had your entree be sure to leave room for dessert. That's my specialty," she says.

"If the main course is as good as these appetizers, I can't imagine having room for anything else." Cleo smiles at her.

A sudden gust of wind blows a flyer across my feet. I bend down and grab it.

"Looks like a storm's coming," Kat says. "How long are you two visiting?"

"We're not sure. We'll be checking out campgrounds."

"The closest one is Fort De Soto. It's only ten minutes away. My girlfriend stayed there before she started parking her motorhome in my backyard."

Despite the heat, I shiver. Could it be JP?

The first drops of rain spatter against the fabric awning above us. The palms start swaying.

"Here comes the storm." I brace myself. I'm starting to

164

get used to these Florida downpours.

"Yes, indeed," Cleo says, staring at the entrance, her eyes wide.

Kat turns to see what's caught Cleo's attention.

"Hi, honey," she says, "come on over and meet my new friends."

I have my back to her, but I know by the look on Cleo's face who it is.

"This is my girlfriend, JP," Kat says as I turn around.

"*Ashley*?" The look of surprise on JP's face is replaced by a look of horror, before she quickly masks it. "Cleo?"

Kat eyes us in complete surprise. "You know each other?"

"What are you doing here?" JP says. Does Cleo or Kat hear the tone of accusation in her voice?

"Looking for you," Cleo says with a smile.

Kat looks from one to the other of us. "But *how*? How do you know each other?"

I turn to face her. "I'm Lizzie's sister." Kat's face looks blank. *She hasn't told her.* I bite my lip and shake my head from side to side in disbelief.

"Lizzie was the name of my ex. The one who passed away," JP says quickly.

"Oh." Kat furrows her brow and I can see her mind working furiously. Had JP mentioned it to her?

"I'm glad you've been able to move on." I try not to sound sarcastic. For now I need JP and Cleo to believe this is truly a welfare visit.

"Thanks." JP looks wary.

Cleo breaks the tension by getting up and giving JP a hug.

"How are you, JP? We've all been so worried about you. Why did you run away like that, without telling us where you were going?"

JP turns to Kat. "I'm sure you have to get back to the kitchen don't you?"

Kat nods, but before retreating she looks from Cleo to me to JP, and shakes her head. JP's going to have some explaining to do later.

I get up and force myself to give JP a hug too. Her body feels stiff against me.

"Join us," Cleo urges JP.

She hesitates, but it's clear she has no excuse not to. She lowers herself into one of the armchairs. Around us, the rain continues to fall, but it's a soft rain, pattering on the palm fronds that surround us.

Cleo leans forward and grasps JP's hand. "It's such a relief to know you're okay. Right, Ash?"

"Of course. But why did you leave like that? Everyone was so shocked. They were your friends."

"It was too hard for me, seeing everyone, being constantly reminded of Lizzie. Even seeing you is hard because you look so much like her."

Cleo nods. "That's true. Though seeing Ash makes me feel like Lizzie isn't completely gone."

"Well she is!" JP bursts out bitterly.

I sit and watch her. Ever since Lizzie died, JP's showed such intense grief. How could it be possible that she was the one who brought about Lizzie's demise if she's so distraught? Her grief seems so genuine that I wonder again whether she made a mistake, that Lizzie wasn't meant to die.

The waitress brings our entrees and JP stands up.

"I'll leave you two to eat. Now that you've found me and see that I'm alright, how long will you stay?"

"I have to get back to work," Cleo says. "Whether or not we found you, I was planning on flying out tomorrow."

"You too?" JP asks, and I don't know if I'm just imagining a hopeful tone to her voice.

"I don't have a job to go back to, so I'm gonna hang out here for a little while. Seems like a nice place to sit and ponder my future."

Cleo stands up and gives JP another hug.

"Give Ash your contact information. We're not going to lose you again."

"I will," JP says. She turns to me. "I expect I'll be seeing you around then."

"I expect you will," I say and smile sweetly.

Chapter Thirty-Three

"Thank you for everything."

We're sitting on the Garrett steps, waiting for Cleo's taxi to arrive and take her to the airport.

"We achieved what we set out to do, didn't we?" I say.

"Yes and no. We found JP." Cleo turns and faces me. "But I had another reason for wanting to be here with you, and I didn't achieve it."

"We're friends, aren't we?" I say, even though my heart is hammering away.

"I want more than that. You know I do."

She takes my hand and strokes my fingers, one at a time. Then she brings it to her mouth and starts kissing each finger in turn. I laugh, despite myself. She pulls me toward her.

"Kiss me goodbye." Her low voice is barely audible and I lean forward.

"Of course," I say lightly.

She takes my face in her hands and puts her mouth on mine. Her lips are soft and firm and when her tongue seeks mine, I don't pull back. I allow myself to feel all the pent-up desire that has been in my body since we first greeted each other in Jacksonville. My legs feel weak and my heart burns with a fierceness I've never experienced before. I should stop, but I don't. One kiss. One goodbye kiss. That's all.

A car honks and we both jump. It's her taxi.

I leap up while she slowly stands and picks up her suitcase, her gaze fixed on me.

She walks down the steps, saying nothing. I watch as she gets in the taxi.

"Cleo—" I run down the steps, but it's too late, the cab

is already moving and she doesn't turn her head as it pulls away from the curb.

I sink down on the steps, my head in my hands, bereft.

"Ashley?"

I look up and see Kat coming into work. I muster up a small wave.

"JP said you're going to stay a few days longer. Cindy says you're welcome to stay at her place."

"Cindy?"

"The waitress who served you yesterday."

"But she doesn't even know me."

"Any friend of JP's is a friend of ours."

I have a feeling she may be waiting for me to explain a little more about our connection or tell her something about Lizzie, but I say nothing.

"Does she rent out rooms? Is it Airbnb or something like that?"

"No. She has extra space at her house and enjoys company."

I'd like to turn down the offer, but the Garrett is expensive and saving money would be very welcome. I thank Kat profusely and she says she'll take me over to Cindy's after work.

ॐ

Cindy's home is a brightly colored bungalow with an enormous yard sheltered by a massive tree with low-hanging fruit. Cindy is out front, sweeping.

"Are those mangoes?" I ask. "How exotic."

"And messy too. They fall and splatter all the time. There are so many I keep the whole neighborhood supplied."

"Thanks for offering your hospitality," I say.

Cindy laughs. "This is Gulfport. It's what we do."

Kat turns back toward her car, ready to leave.

"Enjoy your run tomorrow," Cindy tells her. "I'll miss coming with you."

A pang of excitement zips through me. "You run? May I join you?"

"Sure. Cindy and I usually go together, but she turned

her ankle the other day. I'd welcome company."

🙿

The next morning Kat stops by and we head out. We run by the water and I offer up a silent prayer at the beauty of the sparkling bay. Pelicans dive and swoop, and silver fish jump as if teasing the birds.

We turn up a side street and Kat points things out as we run. "Did you notice that mailbox?" She points to one that's in the shape of a dolphin. "And that tree?" Which isn't a tree at all, but a sculpture made of glass bottles.

The fences are covered with purple and pink bougainvillea and the yards are filled with yellow and scarlet hibiscus. The sabal palms fan us with their fronds and we're shaded by the dappled light that splinters through the enormous oak trees.

We turn again and are back at the water. This time, instead of the view of the bay, it's a marina filled with sailboats.

"Clam Bayou," Kat announces. "Everyone's favorite place to run, sit, fish or make out."

"It's beautiful." The sunlight glints on the water, and a host of birds peck at the grass on the dock. I recognize the pelicans, but there's an enormous prehistoric-looking bird I've never seen before.

"What's that?" I ask, pointing.

Kat stops for a minute, bends over, and puts her hands on her knees to take a breath.

"The large one's a wood-stork. The ones with the long curved beaks are ibis. You'll see them everywhere."

"Amazing."

"JP says you should join her for lunch today. Come to the Garrett. I'll feed you both."

🙿

Now that I finally have time by myself with JP, I feel nervous.

"How did you find me here?" JP breaks small pieces of bread off her roll.

"That was Cleo. She played detective." I haven't

decided how much to tell her about Gail and her friends.

"But why?"

"She and Paula were worried about you."

"But you weren't." She says it as a statement, not a question.

"The house was empty. You obviously had a plan. If you'd been thinking about harming yourself, you wouldn't have gone to all the trouble of selling up first. I was surprised that you left without telling anyone though."

"Like I said, I just wanted to leave it all behind."

"And then I show up." I do my best to look sympathetic. I want to ask her about Lizzie's last day, and the FSGS, and a whole bunch of other questions, but I know it's important to pace myself. I still have a couple of days before I meet with Dr. Patel, so I have time.

"That's okay. Getting away from Philly was the main thing." JP flicks her hand at a fly that's determined to stay on her shirt, however much she swats at it.

"What made you decide to move here?" I ask.

"Serendipity. I didn't have a destination. I met Kat..."

Our conversation is awkward. I can almost feel Lizzie's presence, as if she were sitting on the bench between us. If she were here I would reach out and hold her hand, stroke it just as I did the day she died. I feel a lump in my throat, but I refuse to cry.

"I had to move on." JP has misinterpreted my silence for a judgment.

"Of course." I force myself to add, "Kat seems nice. This town is charming."

"Yeah. Reckon I've fallen on my feet."

I try not to get angry. Here she is, living her life, moving on, while all that's left of my sister is her ashes—if JP even kept them. I remind myself that it's only temporary.

I'm honing in on JP; I can feel it.

Chapter Thirty-Four

JP invites me to walk at Clam Bayou, the nature preserve Kat pointed out on our jog.

"It's not quite the Sierras you love so much, but I figured you'd like it anyway," she says as we walk along the sandy path that takes us to a mangrove-filled bayou.

We sit on a bench opposite the water and look out at the sailboats far in the distance. I want to bring up my idea that JP might have caused Lizzie's death by mistake, but I can't figure out how to start the conversation.

"Why did you really track me down?" JP's direct question surprises me, although it shouldn't. She's always been someone who gets straight to the point.

"I still have so many unanswered questions about how Lizzie died. You left before I could ask them."

JP sighs. "Come on, Ash, put it to rest. I know she was your sister, but she was my wife. If I can let it go, so can you."

"How were you able to let it go? You were so distraught at the hospital and in the days afterward. It was almost as if you blamed yourself in some way."

JP frowns. "Why would I blame myself?"

"Sometimes people feel guilty. They feel as if they could have done something, or maybe they did something they shouldn't have."

"There was nothing I could have done. I told you what happened."

I guess if she did do something by accident she's not going to tell me. At least not for now. "Could you have prevented her from drinking?"

JP looks startled. "I'm not an enabler. You know the only person who can stop a drunk is the drinker."

"I didn't mean in general. But that night...you said she came home drunk."

"So?"

"Well, I'm confused. Because I thought you were together that evening."

"Who told you that?" JP's eyes narrow. I want to get the truth out of her, but I don't want to raise her defenses yet.

"I don't remember. I think it was one of her friends. Said you and Lizzie were on your way to a fancy restaurant. Did you fight on the way there? Is that why you weren't together? Or were you with her when she was drinking?"

"We didn't fight. Yeah...I guess we were together. You probably misunderstood. When I said she went out, I meant like we say in AA, she went out of the program by getting drunk, not that she went somewhere physically."

JP pushes her hair out of her eyes and squints in the bright sunlight.

"If you were with her, why didn't you prevent her from drinking?"

"I didn't realize what was happening until it was too late. And then she got belligerent. Told me I had no right to stop her. You know what drunks can be like."

I don't tell JP that actually I have very little experience with drunks. But I do know my own sister, and describing her as a belligerent drunk has no ring of truth. When she drank with Kurt, she got lighthearted and silly, and later, morose and teary. Lizzie didn't have an aggressive bone in her body.

"I'm confused about the timeline. Helen said you were at the gym that evening and—"

"You talked to Helen about all this?" JP glares at me and her face turns red. "Why would you do that?"

Damn. I wasn't going to let on about Helen.

"We were just chatting. It came up because she mentioned how hard it had been to believe Lizzie was dead, when she'd been at the gym with her just the day before."

"Oh." JP looks a little mollified.

"We were discussing our workouts. She mentioned a class that Lizzie stopped taking after you joined the gym." I wait for JP to say something, but she just stares out at the water. "You never mentioned you'd started going to the gym with Lizzie."

"It never came up. I wasn't hiding it."

JP gets up, and we start walking toward the promontory. From there I can see a bridge spanning the bay far in the distance.

"Here's what I don't understand. She said the class ended at 7:30. You were still in the pool and Lizzie was just starting to get dressed. If that was the case, and then you two went out, when did Lizzie have time to get drunk? Nothing adds up."

"Oh for God's sake, Ashley! Let it go. Why are you going on and on about this?"

"The last time I saw you in Philly I told you why. Lizzie was convinced someone poisoned her. I'm trying to figure out when they could have done it."

"Why do you keep bringing that up? She was probably hallucinating." JP quickens her pace but I can easily keep up with her, however fast she walks. She turns off the path toward the street and kicks at some stones on the side of the road.

"I don't understand why you wouldn't be as anxious as I am to find out if someone killed Lizzie."

"Because I know they didn't. Unlike you, I trust what the doctors tell me."

"Humor me. Help me work it out."

The sun is beating down on us, and it's so humid I'm dripping all over. Why did JP want us to walk in the middle of the day when it's so hot? Nobody else is outdoors. Sweat stains are seeping through her shirt, and she looks as uncomfortable as I feel. Is there a reason why she brought me to such an isolated place surrounded by water?

I pull out a sweat rag from my shorts and start mopping my brow.

"Are you drinking enough?" She offers me her water bottle. I'm touched, if somewhat surprised, by her concern.

"Probably not." Back home I'd have drunk a liter of water if I went for a walk in the midday sun, but it's so humid here, I don't find myself needing to drink at all. She seems to have changed the subject, and I want to return to it. "Won't you help me put this to rest by answering my questions?"

JP sighs, then looks down at her watch. "I need to make a phone call. I can't talk any more right now." She pulls out her phone. "It's easy for you to get back to Cindy's. Just go down that way." She points in the direction we came and starts punching numbers into her phone.

I put my hand on her arm. "I want to finish our conversation, JP."

She looks up, a little exasperated. "I'm on deadline with an article I have to edit." She hesitates then says, "We can go gator-hunting tomorrow. I'll pick you up."

"Day after tomorrow," I say.

Tomorrow I have an appointment in Tampa. With Dr. Patel. And I'm hoping he can help me pull all of this together.

Chapter Thirty-Five

The nine-mile drive across the bridge into Tampa never felt so long as it does today. I try to take in the beauty of the crystal clear water on either side of me and the blue sky   punctuated with a few puffy white clouds, but my mind is focused on the fact that today could change everything. I'm sure Dr. Patel has something fairly momentous to tell me. He wouldn't have me drive all this way, otherwise.

The hotel looks like a white and pink birthday cake set down on a perfectly manicured lawn. I thrust the car keys at a parking attendant, so he can valet park for me, and rush up the steps into the main foyer, two at a time. I cross the expansive reception area and follow signs to the Manzanita Bar, where Dr. Patel said he'd be waiting. It's at the back of the hotel and is part of a lounge filled with white, wicker armchairs and low glass tables. French doors on the far side lead out to a patio. After scanning the room, I walk outdoors where I spot the doctor, sitting by himself in the far corner, close to a bayou where pointy-beaked ibis peck in the shallow reeds.

He stands as soon as he sees me and smiles. "Thank you for coming," he says, "I wasn't sure you would."

"Why?"

"I may have sounded as if I were trying to pick you up, which, although I'm not married, would never be my intention."

His English sounds old-fashioned, but I welcome his sentiments.

I ask him about his conference and whether he's ever visited Tampa.

"Yes, many times. I love it. I've even thought about

moving here." He laughs as if he's told a joke, then explains that physicians from cities like New York and Philadelphia usually consider Florida the Deep South, and not a place to aspire to. "However, I've always enjoyed visiting this area. The mango trees everywhere remind me of my grandparents' estate in Andhra Pradesh."

A waitress approaches to take our drink orders. Dr. Patel orders an Absolut and tonic. "May I buy you one too?"

I've never had one. I generally choose something sweeter, but today's a day for new things. "Yes, thank you. And a glass of iced water with lemon," I add.

The waitress returns with three tall glasses filled with clear liquid, ice cubes and lemon. I only know which the water is because the glass is a different shape.

"Cheers." We clink glasses and I take a small sip of alcohol. I feel it burn the back of my throat, although it doesn't have a strong taste or odor. I have another sip and feel it whack me in the forehead. I decide to take it easy and take a big gulp of iced water.

We fall into an easy pattern of conversation, but eventually I can't wait any longer.

"You said you'd been thinking about Lizzie. You have some ideas?"

"You asked me whether anything would have come to mind if she'd been admitted to the hospital with her presenting symptoms and I didn't know she had FSGS."

"Yes." I hold my breath, waiting for him to continue.

"Your sister had a history of alcoholism as well as FSGS, correct?"

"Yes. She'd been clean and sober for years. JP said she got drunk the evening she brought her to the E.R., but I don't believe it."

Dr. Patel strokes his goatee. "I thought to myself, what if she didn't have FSGS and wasn't drunk, and she presented the way she did? In that case an entirely different idea would have come to mind."

He leans back and sips his vodka. "You understand that this conversation is strictly off the record, don't you? There are no medical facts to back up what I'm about to say. It's just the personal musings of a middle-aged doctor with too much imagination."

"Yes, yes, I get it. Please just tell me."

"Antifreeze." He says the word so softly I must have misheard.

"Pardon me?"

"Antifreeze. It shuts down the kidneys. A person who's ingested it will have slurred speech, confusion and a stumbling gait. If your sister had come in with the symptoms she displayed, and she didn't already have a diagnosis, my first thought would have been that she had ingested ethylene glycol. Otherwise known as antifreeze."

I don't know what I expected to hear, but this wasn't it. "Whoever ingested antifreeze? Isn't that what we put in our cars?"

"Yes. But it's also been used by people who want to commit suicide. In fact, people use it to kill themselves with an alarming frequency."

My drink catches in my throat and I splutter. "My sister didn't commit suicide!"

"How can you be so sure? People who are depressed can hide it very successfully, even to those who are closest to them. She might have been upset about her diagnosis, worried that she'd end up being a burden to the people around her, or scared that she wouldn't get a kidney if she needed it."

It's true; she'd been depressed. But I know what she told me in the hospital. There's no point in holding back, so I tell him what Lizzie said when she was dying. "She was trying to tell me she'd been poisoned."

He raises his eyebrows, but says nothing, so I plow on. "If you'd been there and the idea of antifreeze crossed your mind, would you have ordered blood or urine tests to find out?"

He shakes his head. "This is why I would not tell you anything over the phone, because I will deny we ever had this conversation. You need a very specialized test for ethylene glycol to show up. It wouldn't appear on regular tox screens. Some hospitals have that capacity. We don't. I have been advocating for this improved technology since I joined the hospital, but my chief said it's too expensive. He insists it would be pretty obvious if someone came in with antifreeze poisoning. If we suspect it, the hospital would contract out to do the test."

"But no one did suspect it because of Lizzie's history."

"Exactly."

"So you think she didn't even have FSGS? That somehow someone made it look like she did?"

He shakes his head. "No, I don't think that. Nobody could fake the ongoing history your sister had. But she—or someone else—could exploit her medical history. Antifreeze induces kidney failure and so does FSGS. If she hadn't had that history, it would be a very glaring red flag. And the fact that she also had a history of drinking made it even easier. If someone looks like a drunk, talks like a drunk, and acts like a drunk, we assume that's what they are."

"So even though I can't prove it, and even though you'll deny you ever suggested it, poison by antifreeze is a serious possibility."

He nods slowly. "Although you have no way of knowing who used the antifreeze, or how they used it."

Our waitress approaches and asks us if we'd like refills. I shake my head. "Just another water, please. I'm driving."

Dr. Patel orders another Absolut and tonic then breaks the silence. "There's one thing we haven't accounted for. When I read through your sister's medical record, it stated quite clearly that she was so inebriated that she was still drinking when she came to the E.R. She was reeling from side to side and displaying a flask of vodka for all to see. So you see, even though this terrible idea of poison presents itself, you will have to let go of it and accept that your sister died a very tragic, early death."

Tears spring to my eyes and when the waitress returns, I grab a glass off her tray and take a large gulp before realizing I've picked up Dr. Patel's Absolut instead of my water.

"I'm so sorry for your loss. I'm sure it's hard to accept. But it sounds as if your sister was a delightful person. Hardly one to have made enemies."

"She was," I say. "Everyone loved Lizzie."

"So then, you don't even have a suspect. And even if you did, you don't have a means or a motive."

But he's wrong. Not only do I know who did it and why, I just this moment figured out how.

Chapter Thirty-Six

JP drives us to a place called Mangrove Swamp.

"Did you have a good day yesterday?" she asks.

"Very," I reply, smiling. I'd have preferred to meet with JP in a cozy cafe in the small town of Gulfport, surrounded by people. Instead we've come to a place that's probably popular in winter but seems deserted today.

We head out on a wooden boardwalk that's built over the wetland. The air is humid, the sky filled with threatening dark clouds. An enormous alligator with a crooked smile lazes on the riverbank. JP is even quieter than usual, a brooding expression on her face. A splash startles me, and I turn in time to catch two baby gators sliding into the water. Several smaller ones are sitting on a nearby log, others lying in the mud. They blend in so well I wouldn't even have spotted them. Signs posted along the way remind us that swimming is prohibited. Would anyone be foolish enough to attempt it?

The clouds shift and reveal a blazing sun, and I'm glad of the giant oaks and red maples shading us. The boardwalk ends abruptly and we're facing an open green expanse exposed to a now-burning sun. A trail cuts through it that looks as if it leads to another bayou.

"You okay to keep going?" JP asks.

"I am if you are."

"Here." She holds out a bottle, "I brought some Gatorade for you."

"That's okay. I have my water flask."

"Gatorade's better. If you only drink water, you'll have no energy."

I turn around. "What did you say?"

Overhead a flock of green parrots screech noisily. I've

never seen wild parrots before, but right now I have other things to focus on.

"Lizzie always swore that Gatorade was better than water. She was religious about drinking a bottle after every workout."

"Hmm." Suddenly, I'm miles away.

"Here." JP pushes the bottle at me.

"Maybe later."

The trail is dry and our feet crunch on gravel and dirt. Large osprey perch in the sparse trees that dot the trail, clutching onto branches with their sharp talons.

"You wanted to talk?" It's the first time I've ever made JP so uncomfortable that she starts a conversation, and I'm glad. No more apologizing, no more pussyfooting, I decide to act like JP and dive right in.

"Have you ever heard of Munchausen by proxy?"

JP stops and stares at me. "What the hell is that?"

"Munchausen syndrome is when someone repeatedly makes themselves sick to get attention. By proxy is when they make someone else sick. I read an article about it. Very interesting."

JP looks baffled. "I have no idea what you're talking about."

"I've been going through all the alternatives of what happened to Lizzie. One of them is that someone was trying to make her sick, and keep her sick, but then went too far."

"Are you accusing me of something?" JP stands and faces me. "You think I wanted Lizzie to get sick?" Her eyes are wide, her nostrils quivering. She shakes her head. "You're crazy. I was with her when the doctor diagnosed her with FSGS. I tried to reassure her it was nothing we couldn't handle. She was the one who couldn't deal with it and kept insisting she was going to be a burden on me. She was the one who—" She stops abruptly.

"Who got drunk and had a one-night stand?" I say quietly. "I know that's all the so-called affair was."

She looks surprised. "What do you think? That I manipulated her lab tests? And the blood in her urine? And all the other symptoms she had? You're crazier than I thought."

We've reached the other side of the meadow and are

on an isolated path next to the creek. JP's face is darker than the thundercloud that's moved in above us.
"No. I didn't really think that." I can feel my heart pounding. "I was joking."
JP looks annoyed. "I don't see why it's a laughing matter."
"You told me to lighten up. Guess it wasn't funny. If only I could let go, but there are too many pieces that don't hang together."
"You're obsessed." JP faces me, her eyes narrowed.
"Why wouldn't I be? Lizzie was my only living relative. She was a dear person. I want to know what happened to her."
A noise startles me: the loud splash of a gator. I turn to look at it then sense a movement behind me. I swivel and see that JP has moved closer to me. Much closer. A shiver goes down my spine. Does she want to push me in? If so, I'll damn sure take her with me. I give my head a shake to clear my thoughts. What am I doing out here, anyway, with a woman I think is a murderer? Sweat is trickling down my face and I wipe if off my forehead. "Let's head back."
I keep my eyes on JP as we turn around and walk through the meadow toward the boardwalk.
"Do you have any idea how painful it is for me when you bring up all these crazy ideas about Lizzie?" JP asks. "I loved Lizzie. If anything happened to her, don't you think I'd want to know?"
"Yes, but—"
"But nothing. I know everything I need to—that she was sick, got drunk, and died of kidney failure. You need to accept that, Ash, and move on."
I walk slowly, thinking. "I guess you're right. Maybe it's time to let go."
"It is," JP says. "I'm sorry I didn't answer your phone calls and that I left without telling you. I've been wrapped up in my own grief and couldn't help you with yours. But that's done. From now on, I'm going to be the best sister-in-law you could ask for." She links her arm through mine.
I'm surprised. "Thanks, JP. That means a lot." I pat her hand. "You're right. I will let go. I have to."

"Good for you." The dark expression on JP's face clears, and a look of relief fills her gray eyes.

As we approach the car, I can't help adding, "I just don't know how to put all those questions out of my mind."

"You must have been going crazy. Did you share them with Cleo or anyone?"

"Uh-uh. I didn't want to look like an idiot."

"I expect you've been in touch with her though, telling her about our get-togethers?"

I shake my head. "I don't think Cleo and I will be in touch any more. She—she made a pass at me."

"Wow. Did she ever misread the situation!" JP laughs.

☛

When we're close to Gulfport, I indicate a McDonald's up ahead. "Pull in over there."

"Fast food? You never go to those places. I can take you to a nicer place than that."

"Really. I feel a bit faint. Just pull in."

She does as I ask, and we go to the counter and order sodas. I take them to a nearby table and tell her I need to use the restroom. It's around a corner behind her, so that as I approach it, I can see her, but she can't see me. I stand and watch her for a minute, and when I'm satisfied, I make a quick phone call.

When I return to my seat, she's already slotted the straw into the lid of the soda cup. "Drink," she says. "That'll help you feel better."

"Thanks." I put my mouth on the straw, adjust the lid on the cup, then gulp noisily.

JP sips her drink and we sit for several minutes, not saying anything.

I put my hand to my head. "Actually, I'm not feeling better. I feel dizzy."

"You're probably dehydrated. Have some more of your soda."

I put my lips to the straw and gulp some more.

"You and your sister are a lot alike." JP smiles at me but it's a crocodile smile, never reaching her eyes.

"Oh?"

"You both act holier-than-thou. 'I'm so good. I'm so Christian.'"

"And you think otherwise?"

"Your dear, loving sister betrayed me."

"It was one night. She was upset. And me? What did I do?"

"You asked too many questions."

I shudder. Finally she's going to tell me.

"So maybe it's time for you to answer them," I say, still clutching my forehead and taking some deep breaths. "Did you hate Lizzie in the end?"

"Of course not. I loved her desperately. Especially at the end." JP chokes up.

"And yet you killed her."

JP stares at me. Then she slowly nods her head. "It had to be that way. It was her fault."

I take a deep breath. Let it out. Take another. "You're admitting it. Why now?"

"I want you out of my hair. I figure if I tell you, you'll get out of town."

"Why do you think I won't tell anyone?"

"I'll deny it and you'll sound crazy. You'll never be able to prove anything."

My stomach is in knots. I feel nauseous, but I have to keep going.

"Why was it her fault? Because she was human and made a mistake? She'd just found out she had a chronic illness. Couldn't you cut her some slack?"

"How did I know she wouldn't keep doing it every time the going got tough? You either drink, or you don't drink. You're either faithful, or you're not."

"Why not divorce her?" But I know the answer. I've read enough articles about abusers to know how they feel: *If I can't have you, then nobody will.*

"I couldn't let her go. But I couldn't live with her after what she did. There was no choice."

"So you poisoned her. Tell me how."

JP says nothing. Just stares at me, a smug look on her face. She thinks I haven't worked it out. But she's wrong.

"Okay," I say, "I'll tell you." I pause, then I say slowly and softly, "It was antifreeze, wasn't it?"

JP raises her eyebrows.

"I even helped you throw out the old can when we cleaned up your garage." I shake my head. The irony is not lost on me. "And the part you were even cleverer about was making sure you found a hospital that didn't do the right blood tests. Everyone knows that hospital you took her to is too poorly funded to do expensive testing."

"Not bad, Ash, not bad. You're smarter than you look."

"But just to make certain, you tested out your plan a month earlier. Gave her just a tiny amount. Enough to make her vomit. Then you took her to the hospital and got your answer."

"Impressive. How are you feeling by the way?"

"Not so good. But I'm not done. I know how you did the antifreeze, but Dr. Patel said the hospital notes referenced Lizzie being drunk on admission."

"Dr. Patel? There was no Dr. Patel working there."

"No, but there is now. And he's been very helpful. Although even he didn't put it all together. I had to do that, after I had enough information from him. I kept going over what Lizzie had said that final day. She was trying to tell me that you put the antifreeze in her Gatorade. She said something about water and energy, and I thought she was saying she had no energy. But that wasn't it. She said you put it in her water and then corrected herself and said it was in the energy drink. But I wondered why she had made the mistake of saying water. And that was when I realized how you made it look like Lizzie was drunk when you took her to the hospital. Water and vodka look the same."

JP snorts. "I *was* smart. When I brought her to the E.R., she was stumbling and incoherent and I told them she'd gone on a major bender. She hadn't of course. It was just the effect of the antifreeze. In the truck I gave her a bottle of water to sip on so she wouldn't vomit. Once we were inside the hospital, as she tripped and mumbled and I struggled to hold her up, I switched her bottle with a water bottle filled with vodka. When they asked her what she'd been drinking, she held up the bottle to them and I saw the look that passed between the orderlies: *Friday night and another drunk.*"

I push my hands on the edge of the table, stand up, stumble, and sit back down again. JP drinks the last of her soda and rises.

"You have your answers. I'm going to leave." She smiles at me, a flat smile that goes nowhere. "I do hope you start to feel better. Though I don't think you will." She scrapes her chair back.

"I don't think you're going to leave. Look who just got here."

JP spins around just as Kat walks through the door. JP looks flustered. "Kat? What are you doing here?"

"I was out cycling. I got thirsty."

"Have some of my soda," I say and hold it out to her.

"No!" JP puts herself between me and Kat.

While JP and Kat face each other, I quickly punch numbers into my phone, state my location, and hang up.

"Please," I say, thrusting my drink toward Kat. She leans forward to take it and JP again tries to grab it. I pull it away quickly. "I bet you want it back. The police will have a field day with it. They're on their way right now."

JP lunges toward me and the drink, but Kat is standing between us and she can't reach it.

Kat looks from one to the other of us. "What's going on?"

JP looks scornful. "Come on, Kat, she's crazy. Let's get out of here."

Kat stays where she is. "No, JP. I'm not going anywhere. Not until I find out what this is all about."

"She's sick. Really sick. She's going to collapse any minute."

Kat looks at me and then back at JP. "Why?"

"Because she just drank soda laced with poison."

"*What?*" Kat's eyebrows shoot so high they disappear beneath her bangs.

"She tried to poison me, but I switched our drinks. She's crazy. She's convinced I poisoned her sister, and she wanted to get revenge."

Wow. I have to give her credit for quick thinking. She knows the police are going to find poison in my drink, so she's already trying to put a spin on what's happened. She wants to tell them I'm the one who tried to poison her!

"She doesn't look like she's been poisoned. She seems fine," Kat says, her face showing puzzlement.

JP stares at me. Her face changes color and

her expression goes from shock to confusion. I'm sitting back, my feet propped on the opposite chair. It's quite clear that I'm not dizzy, I'm not vomiting, and I'm not about to collapse.

"I—I don't understand..."

It's the first time I've ever seen JP so completely unsure of herself.

"When you tried to get me to drink the Gatorade this morning, everything fell into place," I say, still leaning back so I can look directly up at her. "I knew you'd poisoned Lizzie with antifreeze, but up until that moment, I hadn't figured out when and how you did it. Then you said you could always rely on Lizzie having her energy drink after the gym. Antifreeze has a slightly sweetish taste, so Gatorade was the perfect disguise. Once I realized that's what you'd used on Lizzie, I was on high alert when you offered me some. I figured if I didn't drink it then, you'd try again later. I needed to be able to prove my theory, so I suggested we come to a fast food place where I knew there'd be security cameras. And I picked a table that would have just the right angle to show you tampering with my drink."

"But you drank it anyway." JP's voice is strangled and her face is ashen.

"No. I placed my fingers on the straw and squeezed it tight so nothing would come into my mouth. Then I gulped to make it look like I was drinking. You couldn't see that the cup was still full. I asked you why you were telling me the truth, and you said it was so I would leave town. In reality, you thought I'd be dead in half an hour and your secret would go with me to the grave." I finish talking just as we hear the sirens. A police cruiser stops outside the front door.

"I'm sorry it ended this way, JP. I know that once upon a time you loved my sister. Now you must live with the guilt of what you've done for the rest of your life."

Chapter Thirty-Seven

Kat and I are seated at a wrought-iron table at the outdoor cafe where Cindy moonlights. The owner is slapping a poster on the window advertising the upcoming Gecko Fest. Pictures of geckos are starting to go up all over town advertising gecko art displays, gecko sculptures, a gecko dance and even a gecko parade.

"I hope you'll stay for that." Kat indicates the poster. "It's such a fun time."

"We'll see," I reply. "I still haven't decided what my plans are."

"Hopefully they include eating a lot of ice cream," Cindy says. She lowers three enormous ice cream sundaes from a tray onto the table and sits down with us.

I look at the massive dessert with a mixture of excitement and horror. I can't remember the last time I've indulged in anything this decadent.

"I'm so grateful to you," Kat says. "I just dread to think what could have happened in the future, if you hadn't made sure JP got caught in the act."

"I'm grateful to *you* that you didn't blow me off when I asked if you'd be willing to drop everything at a moment's notice if I called."

"I got to know you enough that I didn't think you were crazy." Kat smiles and turns her dish around in circles, apparently trying to decide where to start.

"How exactly did you make it all come together?" Cindy shovels her ice cream into her mouth with gusto. I can't help feeling jealous at how she is able to eat with abandon, while I take small spoonfuls and try to make them last.

"I was pretty sure I would need Kat in some way, so

when we went for our run, I put her on alert. Said I might need her at a moment's notice. I'd purposely been trying to rile JP up so she might try something drastic. When I saw Mangrove Swamp, I did worry that JP was planning on feeding me to the alligators, and I wasn't sure there was much I could do about that."

Kat and Cindy look like they're not sure whether or not I'm joking.

"The alligators might well have been part of her plan. If I'd agreed to drink the Gatorade, I'd have keeled over and she could easily have pushed my body into the water. Nobody knew she'd been there with me, so when I was found, they'd have assumed I fell in."

"Surely Kat knew you'd gone there together. Didn't JP borrow your car?" Cindy asks Kat.

"Yes, but she told me she was driving over to Tampa to look into selling her RV. I had no idea she was going to meet Ash."

I dig my spoon into my sundae, throw caution to the winds, and take an enormous mouthful. The mix of vanilla and caramel, chocolate and nuts all swirling in my mouth is heavenly.

"When did you know for sure she was planning to harm you?" Cindy asks.

"When she started asking if I'd said anything to anyone about Lizzie being poisoned. I could have told her that I had, even though it wouldn't have been true. That would have made her think twice about getting rid of me. But I figured if I ever wanted to learn the truth, I had to be willing to put myself at risk. So I told her I hadn't. I even laid it on thick and said I wasn't going to be in touch with Cleo anymore."

I lay my spoon down. Talking about Cleo makes me sad and confused.

"But you will be, won't you?" Kat says.

"I hope so."

Kat smiles. "Maybe sooner than you think."

I pick my spoon back up and dig into my sundae.

"When did you call Kat? And what did you tell her?" Cindy asks.

"I called her after we bought our drinks. I had to leave JP alone with the sodas to give her a chance to doctor mine, so I said I was going to the restroom. I went toward it, but then I turned to see what JP was doing. As soon as I saw her pulling a flask out of her backpack, I called Kat. I asked if she could come into the restaurant in about twenty minutes and tell us she was thirsty."

"I cycled over there on my bike, so by the time I got to McDonald's, I really was thirsty." Kat laughs.

"What did you think was going on?" Cindy asks Kat. "Didn't the whole thing seem bizarre?"

"I had no idea what to expect. Ever since Ashley came to town I started to feel weird about JP. She never told me she had an ex who died or that she'd been married, yet when Ash brought it up, she acted as if I knew and I'd forgotten. I may be flaky sometimes, but even I wouldn't forget something like that! And when I got to the restaurant and saw my car in the parking lot, I knew she'd lied about going to Tampa. So I decided to go along with whatever Ash might say or do."

We slurp up the last of our ice cream, and Cindy says she has to get back to work. I take my wallet out, but Cindy pushes it away. "It's on the house. A small reward for saving the life of my best friend."

"Let's walk up to the Garrett," Kat says.

"Why?"

"I just feel like it." Her eyes crinkle into a smile, and I know there's something she's not telling me.

We walk slowly up the street. "I really do hope you'll move here," Kat says. "Cindy says you can stay with her for as long as you want."

It's tempting. I've been contemplating starting over somewhere new. But I haven't met anyone here who's involved with a faith community, and I'm not willing to let go of that.

As we walk toward the Garrett, Kat starts waving at someone who's sitting on the porch. That's the nice thing about this town; everyone seems to know everyone else. As we get closer, it's apparent the person Kat's waving to isn't someone local. My heart leaps into my throat.

"Cleo?"

She bounds down the steps and runs toward us.

❦

Kat has disappeared and it's just the two of us.

"Let's walk," Cleo says and we take off in the direction of the water.

"I can't believe you're here," I tell her.

"I had to see you. I've been in touch with Kat this whole time. Ever since Gail told me what your suspicions were—"

"Gail told you? You never said."

"I figured it was something you needed to do for yourself. Although I never thought you'd put yourself that close to danger." She links her arm with mine. "I'm glad you're safe."

Her skin resting on mine feels soft and silky. I want to keep it there. I want to walk arm in arm with her everywhere I go, always.

"Why did you tell Gail your suspicions, but not me?" Cleo asks.

"She was a stranger. She could think whatever she liked. I didn't want you to think I was crazy."

"Why would I?"

"Every time we talked about them, you and Paula kept repeating how devoted JP was to Lizzie. I didn't think any of you would believe me."

"Look, if we're going to have a future together, you have to trust me more than that."

"If we're...?" I snatch my arm back. "Cleo, I've told you why I can't."

I move quickly away from her, cross the road, and head toward the water's edge. My heart is pumping furiously. I thought she'd accepted that we would just be friends. Why does she keep pushing for something that's impossible?

She comes up behind me. "No, Ash, you haven't told me the truth. But I figured it out."

The water laps softly at my feet. Gulls fly high above us. I wish I could join them, soar above the earth instead of have to deal with what's going on right in front of me.

"You told me you were nineteen years old when your parents died." Cleo stands next to me at the water's edge.

"Yes."

"So you were in college?"

I nod.

"And when you were in college, you had a girlfriend. Right?" I stare out at the water and remember two college girls, so happy, so excited. Even though they knew what they were doing was wrong. "In your mind, those two things are connected, aren't they? Your college sweetheart and your parents' death." I sink to my knees into the sand, almost as if I'm praying. Tears start to fall down my cheeks. "It's not just in my mind," I choke out. "It's much more than that. I called my parents and asked them to come to campus. I was going to tell them about me and Sarah. I didn't want to wait until I went home at the end of the semester. The accident they were killed in? It was all because of me. If I hadn't been planning to tell them about Sarah, they never would have been in the car that day on their way to see me." I'm sobbing now, the tears streaming down my face. For a moment I remember JP, how she cried, wailed and screamed after Lizzie died, and it's what I want to do too. I feel the same way she must have: desperately sad and wholly guilty.

Cleo folds me in her arms, and this time I allow her to hold me. "Even Lizzie didn't know they were on their way to see me," I whisper through my tears. "I thought she'd never forgive me if she knew."

"You never gave her the chance. Lizzie would have forgiven you because she'd have known there was nothing to forgive."

"But—"

She puts her finger on my lips to hush me. "I don't think she'd have thought for a moment you were responsible. Even if she did, she'd have forgiven you. Just as you should forgive yourself. You're a Christian. You know how important forgiveness is."

"Forgiveness of others..." I mumble, though my tears are starting to subside. It does feel good to finally tell someone the secret I've lived with all these years.

"You thought your parents were killed because you were gay? God wasn't punishing you. It was a terrible   accident. How could you think that? You know what the Bible says: children aren't punished for the actions of their parents, and neither are parents for their children. And anyway, there was nothing to be punished for. You did nothing wrong. Look around you, Ash. There are good, gay people everywhere, doing amazing things in the world. And unfortunately there are a few bad apples too, like JP."

She looks serious, but there's compassion in her expression too. "You walked around with all that guilt, and then a few years later, Lizzie came out. No wonder you had a hard time with it."

"I tried to warn her. I told her God would punish her, but she just laughed it off. For a while I thought maybe she was right. But now..."

"No! You weren't being punished, and neither was Lizzie. She was living her life the way it was supposed to be lived. Your sister knew who she was, and deep down, you know who you are too. You've known ever since college. The sin will be if you try to live the life of someone you're not."

"How can you be so sure about all of this?" I look up into Cleo's eyes. "Weren't you also taught it was wrong?"

"You better believe I was. But the world has changed. Even the church has changed. Do you know how many welcoming churches there are now? You don't have to belong to one that's stuck in the past."

Is it true? Could I really be with her and still be devoted to my faith?

Cleo takes my face in her hands and brushes the tears from my eyes.

"I'm not going to expect you to change overnight. But I am going to help you open those beautiful eyes to the truth." She kisses my eyelids, softly, gently. "If you'll let me." She turns my face up to hers and her lips brush mine.

"I'll let you," I say and put my lips back on her mouth. Only this time I do more than just brush them. I lean in, let her mouth envelop mine, and savor her taste on my tongue.

She pulls me close and I feel the electricity fly between us, sparks that ignite a fire in my belly. I feel the flame of desire rising. For one brief moment an old tape plays in my head: *it's the fire of damnation*. But the moment is so brief it barely registers. What registers is that there's a woman in this world willing to accept me, baggage and all, and that all I need to do is accept myself.

For the first time since I was nineteen, I believe I can do that. With Cleo by my side, anything is possible.

Also Available from Alison R. Solomon

Along Came the Rain

Wynn Larimer would be the first to admit she has a bad memory and that lately it's been getting worse. But that doesn't explain how she has ended up in jail, accused of kidnapping two teenage foster kids. Now she's in the fight of her life to clear her name. Her burning question: who has framed her and why?

Wynn's partner, Barker, is hanging by an emotional thread. Not only are the missing girls her social work clients, but to make matters worse, her beloved Wynn seems to be losing her mind. How can she ensure the girls are brought to safety while dealing with a partner who is increasingly scattered?

Wynn and Barker must race to uncover the truth before Wynn is charged with a serious crime that could imprison her for years. But what will happen to their relationship when both discover things about each other that will change their lives forever?

Sapphire Books, 2016.

ISBN (Print) 978-1-943353-27-9
ISBN (E-book) 978-1-943353-28-6

Available at all major ebook retailers.
Keep up on Alison's latest news and projects:

www.AlisonRSolomon.com

Follow Alison on Twitter @AlisonRSolomon

If you enjoyed this book, please consider posting a review on Amazon, Goodreads and your own social media pages.

65859780R00121

Made in the USA
Charleston, SC
06 January 2017